TIME HUNTER

THE TUNNEL AT THE
END OF THE LIGHT

TIME HUNTER

THE TUNNEL AT THE END OF THE LIGHT
by STEFAN PETRUCHA

TELOS
.CO.UK

First published in England in 2004 by Telos Publishing Ltd
61 Elgar Avenue, Tolworth, Surrey, KT5 9JP, England • www.telos.co.uk

Telos Publishing Ltd values feedback. Please e-mail us with any comments you
may have about this book to: feedback@telos.co.uk

ISBN: 1-903889-37-5 (paperback)
The Tunnel at the End of the Light © 2004 Stefan Petrucha
ISBN: 1-903889-38-3 (deluxe hardback)
The Tunnel at the End of the Light © 2004 Stefan Petrucha
The moral rights of the author have been asserted.

Typeset by TTA Press
5 Martins Lane, Witcham, Ely, Cambs, CB6 2LB, England • www.ttapress.com

Printed in England by Antony Rowe Ltd
Bumpers Farm Industrial Estate, Chippenham, Wilts SN14 6LH

1 2 3 4 5 6 7 8 9 10 11 12 13 14 15

British Library Cataloguing in Publication Data.
A catalogue record for this book is available from the British Library.

TIME HUNTER

THE TUNNEL AT THE END OF THE LIGHT
by STEFAN PETRUCHA

PROLOGUE

Sometimes, huddled against the scratchiness of a rocky corner, my swollen belly hurting with emptiness, my hairy skin cold save for the fast, hot breath and body warmth of the others, I calm myself enough to dwell on myself. And my mind, sensing my mind, can reflect on certain truths, such as:

These are not words. I have no words.

I have aches and pains, longings and absences. I have hungers, lusts, limbs and teeth – but no abstract symbols to codify and echo these things. I have sound. I can howl to the others about food, or danger, or the need for sex, but that's all.

Or: There is no light. I have no light.

To call it dark is meaningless. There never was any light. I don't even know how I can guess at the idea. Maybe my dreams extrapolate it from the three shades of grey I sometimes see, or maybe I imagine that the twin orbs in my head were not always so useless as they are now. Why have them, then, to begin with? Why place them so prominently? They barely tell me anything, but they're always swollen with tears, stinging, and I feel, or know, or guess, that directly behind these large, obsolete orbs lies the most crucial part of my being.

I wonder many things. I don't know about the others, but I am aware that I'm aware, and I wonder why that is. I wonder why they don't seem to think or see, and why it hurts to think that, why my heart wants so badly that the wetness comes again and again to my useless orbs, even when my belly is full and I am warm.

Maybe it's not so bad. Maybe it's me.

The others seem satisfied. Things sting, tickle, bite, scratch. Rough or soft or in between. They hit the ears, drip and echo, screech and whisper. Tongue tastes grit, bitter roots, squishy fish in oily water. There is little else to speak of, except perhaps for the feel of us. Of each other. Pointy, bony frame to pointy, bony frame, skin flapping over bone like a half-sheared pelt. Yet there is the strength of granite in our limbs.

But that's all. All the category. All the sense. All the shade. All the distinctions to be made in the world. Except, oh yes. The sweetness.

Sometimes, oh sometimes, such a rare, rare sometimes, it is like birth or death; I find among the things I feel a heavenly sweetness, and pull it to my tongue. And then all is tickled and alive, and the darkness dances with laughter.

Heaven lasts a moment. The others always smell it. They read me the way they do the heat or the coolness of the rocks or the odours that the air drafts carry. They know when I have sweetness. They even know when I'm about to find it, sometimes before I know myself.

And so, after a moment's joy, there is the scratching, the pulling, the tearing, to get it away from me. It is torn and shredded, passed from hand to hand as far as it will go. It never goes very far without vanishing, for we are many and we all have teeth.

Some are killed for holding on too long. If the sweetness does not move fast enough, a head crushed by stone, or body scratched too deeply to recover. Then they are eaten the way a rat is, or one of the Meaty Ones that sometimes wander down here with the strange pelts that cover their skin.

I learned quickly not to hold on too long. They thought enough not to kill me, because I am best at finding such things, but they hurt me, hurt me badly, and unlike them, I learned.

That was the first time I realised I was different; when I knew I had learned not to hold on too long. It was also when I first felt free to hate them all, myself with them, to hate them for their nearness, for the yowls, for their sharp fingers, for their teeth, for their smells, for the way they dumbly follow me, because I am better at finding the sweetness. And to hate myself for being in the world with them – and wonder where it is that the Meaty Ones come to us from, and if it is any different.

So, before I sleep, I let my mind sense my mind. But when I wake, I am looking. The others think I search for sweetness, but my thought is on the

Meaty Ones, and where they come to us from. If they can wander here, perhaps I can wander there. So instead of searching for sweetness, I scour the cracks and crevices to find a way away. To the others, it looks just the same.

But if ever I should find such a way, I must not let them know. We are as much in each other's minds as we are in each other's way, and, by and by, they would find me. They would be terrified to lose me. They would kill and eat me rather than lose me. So, instead, if I find such a way, I must hide it, even from myself, and wait until I find some sweetness. Then I can give it to them, and while they are in heaven, I will go away.

Where is there to go? My mind thinks a place different than this, where I am not surrounded and used, where my eyes are not useless. But I have no idea what it would look like or how to get there, or even if the journey would take more than I have life to give.

But that matters little.

I have no sense of time.

CHAPTER 1

These scenes are always wet, Lt Clive Gidley mused, spitting a bit of mud away from his upper lip. Muck-brown water, with the occasional chunk of mud, continually splashed into his face, its source an unseen leaking pipe that someone had forgotten to seal. Despite the discomfort, he didn't blame the work crew for clearing out as soon as they could.

The mad thing to do was remain, with a doodlebug between one's legs.

He wiped his face and shifted, hoping to better secure his precarious balance. His manicured hand sunk into mud, making him nearly slip before he could yank it free. At that, his strong, steady heart skipped a beat.

Best not try that again, he thought. *Think about the girl.*

A pretty thing. He'd almost met her at the pub the other night. Ever since, his thoughts wandered back to the wistful moment she had risen from, then vanished back into the crowd. She'd had the kind of red hair that glowed blonde at the highlights. When she'd seen him looking, just before she'd disappeared, she'd smiled in a way that made him smile back. Just thinking about her made him smile again.

There, that calmed him enough to continue. With the right attitude, he might even parlay his fear into indignation. Indignation always made him more competent. So he began thinking how unfair it was for him to be here stuck in the muck of a deep tunnel just adjacent to an unused, *ghost*, station on the Piccadilly Line.

Bad enough this silly buzz bomb had somehow lodged itself way down here. Worse still was the fact that once a routine tube inspection brought it to light, it was quickly deemed too close to the old station simply to blow it up with a half pound block of TNT, as they usually did in such cases. Apparently, old Constitution Hill station, somewhere between Green Park and Hyde Park Corner, closed since 1934, was more valuable than the life of one lieutenant.

Oh, he'd guessed the reason, even though they wouldn't tell him. He knew, from the bricked up walls he'd passed on his way in, that the station must have had a military use during the War. They'd always picked the 'deep level' lines – dug in at around 220 feet – and this was one. There were probably classified files stored in classified file cabinets in the classified station. And that was why he was at risk.

There were scratches in the coloured paint along the body, revealing the metal shell, indicating perhaps it had slipped from its original point of impact. That was a good sign. The igniters could be so damaged, or faulty, that the thing would never go off. That was typical of the FZG-76, or V1. V for *vergeltung*, retribution, supposed payback for the bombing of German urban areas. Unfortunately, also typical of the V1s were an electrical impact igniter and two mechanical ones, which made defusing the thing terribly difficult.

What colour had her dress been?

Light, not white, but close to it, crumpled at the neck and sleeves. It had hung loosely on her slight frame, popping out here and there when it encountered some rounder flesh. Local girl, likely. She'd been there before and would be there again.

And she'd smiled at him.

And why not? He deserved a smile. He'd been chosen for this little task because he was the best. In fact, he'd been part of the team that had defused a V2 on 22 March 1945. One of three failed V2 impacts that had occurred during the course of the War. In that case, the warhead had been on the ground. Defusing it, despite the lack of practical experience, had been relatively easy. V2s were not expected to fail, and seldom did. V1s were not so easy.

Stethoscope firmly in his ears, its business end stuck tightly to the bomb, he twisted the screwdriver just a bit, trying for steady, even, pressure.

Make it as natural as gravity, his instructor had told him, six years earlier.

Easy enough to say. One ton of explosives could flatten a city block.
Think about the girl.

She was slight, pretty, but in a very shy kind of way – and he knew she had really smiled at him. She probably wouldn't even mind the shake in his right hand. It would probably make her love him even more. Sacrificed his health for England, and all. And it wasn't really all that much of a shake. Acted up mostly when it was damp. Like now.

He applied a touch more pressure. The metal creaked, just a bit, and he caught a flash, in his mind's eye, of swirling debris hurtling up into the sky.

Think about the girl.

Sweet eyes. Thin lips.

The plate came loose in his hands. He was more than halfway home now, more than halfway back to the girl. More than halfway . . .

Out of time.

Things had been lonely after the war. He'd never been very good at meeting people. Wasn't gregarious, a quality he envied. But being in a pit below the earth with a bomb, if nothing else, set your priorities straight, so he vowed there'd be no more lonely drinking. He'd finish this job, then head back to the tavern and go on up to her. He'd even have a grand story to tell.

He could even tell her about the V2. He'd received a medal for that! He could explain, he was sure, in an engaging tone, how the fall of a V2 rocket was a series of events that took place in a kind of jangled time. Unlike the V1, the V2 travelled faster than the sounds it made – three times the speed of sound, to be precise. As it was about to hit, if you were unlucky enough to be standing nearby, you'd hear a whip-cracking sound. This was the blast wave created by the explosion. That wave would hit the ground first, before the rocket, a split second before the bright flash of impact. This would be followed by the sort of chaos you'd expect from a huge explosion. But *then*, oddly, ironically, like a ghost of the moment gone, you'd also hear a whine and a rush of whistling air, as the sound of the rocket's coming caught up with the rocket itself. The only warning you got, Gidley could tell her as her eyes went wide, was after the fact.

Out of time.

But it wasn't like that now. This was a V1, and it wasn't going anywhere at any speed. So here, snug in his dripping pit, when his hand moved to the far left, perhaps in a subconscious effort to wipe some of the collected sweat from his brow, Gidley could hear a little crackling spark as the electrical igniter went off.

Not before, or after, just *as*.

As the payload exploded, just before it made Lt Gidley a very small part of a two hundred foot hole in the ground, it occurred to him that perhaps he shouldn't have been thinking about the girl at all.

In the same spot the next day, paunchy, thick-haired and generally jolly Chief Engineer Whit closed his eyes a moment to savour without distraction the taste of chocolate in his mouth. Someone had once told him that chocolate made the human brain react the same way as being in love. A confirmed bachelor for many years, much as he delighted in the company of the ladies, Whit had long ago decided he preferred chocolate.

But, there was a time for pleasure and a time for business, and the sooner he got his business done here, the sooner he'd be back to his pleasure. So, swallowing and stuffing the bar back in his shirt pocket, he opened his eyes, held up his electric torch and took a good, long look at the hole the previous day's blast had left.

'Look at that, would you?' he said, to no-one in particular.

Within minutes of the explosion, the standby emergency crews had swarmed into the area, buttressing this and propping up that, and though they'd done a fine job of it, it still looked like a lot of sad, fragile latticework pressed against a very big hole in the ground – a much bigger hole than even a ton of explosives should have made. It seemed to go on forever, like a cavern.

Whit reasoned that the blast had opened up some sort of neighbouring air pocket, and that at least half of what he was looking at had been there, concealed by a relatively thin wall of rock, long before the V1 had ever made it down to these depths.

From what he could make out of the blast radius itself, most of it had extended down along a path of least resistance, through softer rubble, leaving the concrete supports of the underground train tunnel relatively intact. In fact, it looked like even if any sort of cave-in were to occur, the folks living above had little to worry about.

Sticking his torch in his mouth, he unrolled some blueprints in the dim yellow light, to confirm what he recalled. He was right: the survey maps showed no additional construction beneath the ghost station. So whatever had been opened up was natural in origin, or at least more than a few hundred years old. He stepped forward towards the large opening, the pale yellow light of his electric torch a sad candle against the darkness within. It was his duty to enter – he had to make sure there were no structures there, or at least try to judge if the opening extended under the tube. That might cause some additional trouble.

Slowly, half sitting on broken rock, half walking, he made his way a few feet down and in. Leaning low, he saw that the hole seemed to veer off further down and toward the east, like a tunnel. This was good news, since that direction was away from the track. Better news, there wasn't a man-made object in sight.

He was just about satisfied that his inspection was complete, when he heard something shift. Whit was well aware that human hearing wasn't quite so good at placing the location of sounds in the lower registers, but he guessed the noise had come from further down. Probably some rock settling, but it might be dripping water, which could ultimately cause a collapse. Better make sure.

Eyes closed, he took another bite of chocolate, then slipped further in and down. The sound came again. Rock against rock? Certainly *something* against rock.

He swung his torch around in time to catch something moving. A shadow flitting just out of his vision. Now, that wasn't a rock. One of the men having some fun with him? Whoever it was would have to be barmy to risk the climb down here for the sake of a joke. That meant it could be only one person.

'Chester?' he called out into the dark.

Then, all at once, it wasn't just one sound anymore, or one shadow. It was a dozen. The sounds built into a cacophony of scraping, and below that a strange hiss that bore a vague resemblance to human breath. The shadows were moving so quickly, falling into one another, it was impossible to tell what they were.

He turned to run, but bony hands, strong, quick and eager, pulled him down on his back. The torch slipped from his grasp, its beam revealing patches of filthy, hairy skin as it rolled, and occasionally the most horrid eyes and teeth. His chocolate bar was wrested from his hand by forces unseen, and seemed to float away in the darkness, carried aloft invisibly with shrill whines of delight.

A thought struck him, that maybe the confectionary was all these things wanted, and that now they'd let him go. It was a childish thought, though. Pain tore through his right leg. His arms flailed about helplessly.

The last thing he saw was the torch, having rolled against a rocky wall, illuminating an oblong circle of yellow and grey.

The last thing he heard was the sound of something chewing on his leg.

CHAPTER 2

Time present and time past are both perhaps present in time future, and time future is contained in time past.

Honoré Lechasseur had read that somewhere, recently. On the street, he'd picked up a yellowing, coverless volume from a cardboard bin full of old books, only to read that first line and toss it back with a smile. He had nothing against poetry, but he'd been looking for something to help take his mind off things. While it may have been a lovely metaphor for the human condition, for him it was quite literal.

Aged twenty-nine, jet black hair prematurely greying, he looked from the filthy window of his North London flat and saw a matchstick in a tall woman's fingers spark, burst into flame and rise to the end of her cigarette, all before she even removed the matches from her purse.

As if possessed of an invisible second set of eyes, Lechasseur was forever seeing past and future events. Not in simple visions, either. They spiralled out, like the spinning lights of whirligig rides at amusement parks. If he paid attention long enough, or failed to banish the inciting sight from his mind, they left long, gooey trails that reminded him, for some grotesque, boyhood reason, of worms. They were like living things, some a few feet long, some stretching off to the horizon, twirling as the earth moved.

They were patterns, these worms; happenstance born of the of the physical world, but still intangible truths. Unfortunately, a solid sense of the distinction between the worms, which he considered *there*, and the present day he inhabited, which he considered *now*, had yet eluded him, and Lechasseur, in his dark moments, of which there were many, often feared that he himself was *there* and not *now*.

Hence the books that lined the nooks and crannies of his spartan flat. Lechasseur was fond of sitting and reading in the gloom, where there were fewer things outside of him that could move. To that end, he usually kept the curtains – just thick, torn blankets, really – drawn tight. No such luck today, though. Today, they were boldly open, allowing the unwelcome light and smells of the misbehaving world to intrude brazenly on his mind. A wrinkled old woman folded into a foetus. A child grew into a successful businessman. A poodle being walked by a hasty fellow was strangled to death, its body hidden in a park. He could see its flesh rot into the earth, leaving only the skeleton. It was maddening.

'So, it's not so bad, then, is it?' Emily Blandish called cheerily from what passed as the kitchen area. It was thanks to her that the window was uncovered. She'd been fed up with his sulking of late and decided to do something about it.

Fearing she'd read his mind, Lechasseur pretended he didn't know what she meant and furrowed his brow. Surprisingly, she nodded towards the sun: 'The weather. You put up such a fuss about opening those dingy curtains. You know, people need sunlight to be healthy. You could be depressed just because you're in the dark all the time.'

And here he was thinking just the opposite. Sensation depressed him. Still, Emily had her own mind, full of the most odd bits of information, and he admired her for it. Admiration aside, though, he was starting to wish she had her own mind somewhere else. Her constant presence was a drain. He'd never realised, until her arrival, how much he needed regular solitude in order more easily to face his days.

But now they were linked, not by sex or by romantic love, but by friendship, and the inescapable fact that while he was what was called a time sensitive, she was a time channeller; while he could see time, she could actually move through it. Every now and again, they'd run into someone whose time-line seemed a bit off. If he and Emily touched one another as they thought the same thing . . . whoosh, there and then became here and now – and they'd be stuck in another time, until they could find a way back. They'd met under strange circumstances. She'd just appeared in London, an amnesiac in pink pyjamas, and he'd helped her because it was something he'd needed to do. After that, they'd stayed together as friends, bonded by their complementary abilities as well as by a mutual respect for each other.

As he watched sundry Londoners rushing to and fro, and saw, in advance, where they were rushing to, and where they had rushed from, Lechasseur had a wry premonition that it would be raining soon. He thought of sharing it with Emily, but she was onto other things – reading the paper, humming some tune she recalled from her forgotten past – and he decided it might be cruel to interrupt the chain of recollections.

As if feeling his attention on her, she stopped, turned to him and said: 'What did you think I meant?'

He grunted, not wanting the conversation that would ensue. After all, he'd thought she was talking about time travelling. Lechasseur didn't mind the danger so much – he'd seen action in the War, and some more since as he tried to make his way in post-War London – but the travelling itself was an exacerbated form of the disorientation he felt whenever he caught a glimpse of a timeline. Each time, as of yet, he worried it would drive him mad.

He also knew he was the only available key – or potential key – to the mystery of Emily's identity. It seemed likely, at least to the two of them, that it wasn't just a question of *where* she came from, but *when*. As a result, she was always pushing Lechasseur – gently, mostly – to explore their abilities further. He was sympathetic, but the subject brought up an animal-like survival instinct that he'd yet been able to control.

So, instead of answering, he decided simply to stand by the window and enjoy what he could of the view. By and by, no doubt guessing exactly what had been on his mind, she went back to her humming. The song, a cheery tune, without any words, made him smile. It was the last smile he'd experience for quite some time.

A knock came at the door. The sound was so soft, yet insistent, that Lechasseur thought the caller must be a child. Perhaps some mother had sent her daughter along to express dissatisfaction with some black market meat he'd provided. He didn't think that could be it, though; he was careful to check all the goods that passed by him.

As Lechasseur headed to the door, he saw Emily lower the paper and look up. It was only then that he noticed the headline: THIRD HUMANOID

ATTACK NEAR BLAST CENTRE. Wondering what that could mean, he hesitated and was about to ask, but the knocking increased in intensity.

'All right, I'm coming!' Lechasseur said as he pulled open the door. Then, all he could think was: *A toad. This man is a toad.*

Not a small one, either. Lechasseur had in mind a big, warty bull toad of the sort he used to catch as a child in the swamps outside New Orleans. Some had been so large, he had been barely able to get the fingers of his two hands around them. The fellow at the door was bigger, of course: a few inches over five feet, round, wearing sunglasses and a full suit much too heavy for the weather. He stood outside the door, looking left and right with big round eyes. Lechasseur nearly laughed. He was like something out of a child's picture book. He also caught the thick, sweet odour of the man's cologne.

The effect on Lechasseur and Emily was instantaneous. There was definitely something strange about him – not only in his appearance, but in his very being. They'd experienced the sensation previously, but this time it was positively overwhelming – and neither could keep from staring. Lechasseur imagined they must look fairly animal, for, seeing their eyes, their visitor immediately took two wobbly steps back from the threshold.

'Sorry, wrong. Must be wrong . . . ' he squeaked, looking fairly terrified.

Lechasseur struggled to get a hold of himself and said: 'No, wait, please. Who are you looking for?' By then, Emily was at his side, joining her eyes with his. He could feel her body itching to reach out and touch the strange man.

He also expected at any moment to see the worms start reeling from him, showing in cryptic flashes the source of the disturbance. But nothing came, only an image of darkness. A voice in the back of Lechasseur's head said: *Touch him. Touching helps you see.*

As if acting of its own accord, Lechasseur's hand shot out to grab the visitor. Shocked, the stranger lurched backwards and nearly fell.

'Mistake, mistake. I'm sure of it,' the toad-man said, catching his balance and taking a few more quick steps back.

'I'm Honoré Lechasseur,' was all Lechasseur could think to say.

The man stopped short, blinked twice, then squinted. There was now some distance between them. Emily, as if hypnotised herself, tried to step forward, but a quick nudge from Lechasseur stopped her cold.

'You're spiv, then?' the man asked cautiously, as if it were a name, not an occupation. Lechasseur nodded slowly, as if trying to coax a deer from the woods. Without turning toward her, he added: 'This is Emily Blandish . . . my friend.'

Moving awkwardly, the man pulled a handkerchief from his pocket and dabbed the moisture from his face. It was only then that Lechasseur noticed how profusely the newcomer was sweating. No wonder, given his clothing. But Lechasseur had the strangest sense that it wasn't the heat that was the cause. Moreover, the man's swollen flesh seemed to hang rather loosely on his skeleton; again, like the meat on the leg of a toad.

The man stiffened and gave a quick bow that Lechasseur thought for a moment might be a Germanic affectation.

'Randolph Crest, sir. They say spiv can help with a . . . a predicament . . . most unusual.'

Lechasseur nodded. 'Come in. Let's talk.'

A few seconds passed before Lechasseur realised that neither he nor Emily had moved an inch to let the man in. He pulled Emily back into the flat, giving Crest a wide berth to enter.

With surprising ease of movement, Crest came in, then manoeuvred along the wall. When Lechasseur took a step towards him, pretending it was an innocent gesture, Crest twisted and turned to avoid even so much as a glancing contact. Lechasseur knew that physical contact might reveal the man's history to him, but surely Crest had no idea of that?

In a few more steps, during which the only sound was the rustling of Crest's too-heavy coat, the toad-man reached the windows and immediately pulled the curtains, blocking out the sunlight.

'Apologies. Apologies. Sunlight disturbs,' he said. He seemed about to relax just a bit when Lechasseur, again compelled by such a strong instinctual desire to learn more about this man that it overcame his natural fear, used the pretext of adjusting the curtains to make a further attempt to brush against Crest. The effort was awkward, amateurish and obvious.

Crest whirled, in a fury, and made for the centre of the room. Emily and Lechasseur immediately stood, arms and legs akimbo, as if, should he try to flee, they would have to try to catch him.

With that, Randolph Crest flushed bright red and screeched: 'Would you mind not trying so hard to *touch* me?' It was apparent that he'd wanted to bellow, but his voice simply wasn't equipped for it. 'It's terribly *obvious*, you know! Don't think I can't tell!'

'I'm . . . I'm sure I don't know what you mean,' Lechasseur said, backing away.

Panting and wheezing, Crest stood in the middle of the small room, wide-eyed, slightly hunched, as if ready to fight physically for his privacy. 'I am . . . have . . . among other conditions . . . aphenphosmphobia. Fear of physical contact. As a child I was touched, too much, too often, and now cannot bear it!'

Emily and Honoré exchanged embarrassed glances.

'I understand, and I'm sorry, Mr Crest. It won't happen again. I promise. I'll just take a seat here. Miss Blandish will sit by the window,' Lechasseur said in a slow, deliberate voice.

Before Crest could answer, Lechasseur did as promised and sat in an old, torn reclining chair he'd rescued from an alley rubbish pile. As if to show he had no weapons, he also placed his hands firmly on the chair's thick arms. Emily, as if hypnotised, stumbled backwards until she reached a plain wooden chair. She plopped herself down, then folded her hands neatly in her lap.

Crest watched each movement eagerly. After a few moments, he exhaled, and his bulging eyes seemed to shrink just a bit.

'Perhaps . . . perhaps I misjudge. I have so few choices,' he said, pulling his handkerchief again from his inside pocket and dabbing the patina of sweat from his forehead. Lechasseur noticed that the handkerchief was monogrammed, RC. He also caught another whiff of what he thought was cologne, but briefly wondered if Crest's sweat itself was somehow perfumed.

'Please don't worry, Mr Crest. What was it you thought I might help you with?' Lechasseur said, trying to seem businesslike.

'Word is that in these days of rationing and poor necessity distribution, spiv can obtain things,' Crest said, ending with a nearly girlish giggle.

Lechasseur's response was standard. He shrugged and said: 'Maybe.'

The handkerchief came out again, more sweat was dabbed off. 'I'm a poet, Mr Lechasseur, nearly twenty years now. I have reputation and influence.'

Emily furrowed her brow. '*That* Randolph Crest? I was reading about you a month or so ago. *The Darkness That Hides as Kind*? Was that yours?'

Crest smiled a bit at having been recognised, then nodded in a gesture of practiced graciousness. 'Yes, yes. So, you know. As such, I have certain connections that have indicated that spiv is much more than merely a spiv.'

Emily tensed. Lechasseur remained noncommittal.

'Maybe,' Lechasseur repeated, wondering if he'd given up too much, but unwilling to let the conversation hit any roadblocks. For Crest, the verbal wink was as good as a nod.

'Then I'll be to the point,' Crest said. He leaned forward, a tiny bead of sweat accumulating at the tip of his roundish nose. 'They think they know me, and because of what they think they know of me, they want to kill me.'

'Who want to kill you?' Lechasseur asked.

Crest shivered and lowered his forehead to his hand. 'As if my poem were made flesh and now sought to destroy its creator.'

'I'm sorry?' Lechasseur said.

Crest grew more tense. His hands clenched and his thumbs desperately rubbed the loose white flesh of his index fingers.

'The paper of today, you have it? You know of the attacks?' he said.

Lechasseur shook his head, but Emily spoke up again. 'The sub-humans they say attacked that guard in the underground? By the blast site? You think they want to kill you?' Her disbelief was made plain by her expression. 'Why?'

Crest tapped the side of his head, sending a few barely-perceptible drops of sweat from his black, oily hair down the side of his pasty cheek. 'Everyone has gifts. Spiv and you have yours. Mine is to have dark creatures in my head. They're not so much real as they are nightmares, fed by my own passions, the darkness inside me I can't control. Don't you see? I'll keep on giving them power until they use it to destroy me.'

The reference to gifts was disturbing. How much did he know about them? Still, Lechasseur said nothing, he simply stared and hoped that Emily would realise she should keep up the questions.

Taking the hint, Emily asked: 'Um . . . why not go to the police?' But she was thinking, *or a psychiatrist?*

Crest barely moved as he answered. 'Like you, they'll think I'm insane. But I'm hopeful that, unlike them, you'll see that there's more.'

A silence ensued. When Lechasseur realised that Emily could think of nothing further to ask, he said: 'I suppose we could look around, ask some questions. Then there's the matter of my fee . . .'

Before Lechasseur could continue, Crest lobbed a crumpled envelope into his lap, as if tossing raw meat to a tiger. It was thick with money.

'For the preservation of my life, Mr Lechasseur. I hope it will be enough.'

With that, Crest rose, never once taking his eyes from both Emily and Lechasseur. 'My card is in the envelope as well. I trust you will be in contact.'

As they remained seated, he cautiously backed toward the door and let himself out.

No sooner had the door closed than Lechasseur turned to Emily, to find a knowing expression on her face.

'Well, don't look at me! You were trying to touch him, too!' she protested.

'I know, I know!' Lechasseur answered, hands up in surrender. 'There was just something about him . . . something very strange.' He laughed a bit at himself. 'Perhaps even more than the obvious! He practically glows. You looked mesmerised yourself. Could you tell anything?'

Lechasseur knew there were times when Emily had a sort of second sight about people, not as specific as his visions, but she often caught a sense of people that slipped by him.

'English isn't his native language, but I think anyone might be able to tell that much. If I remember what I read correctly, he's considered a minor talent, but utterly mad, even certifiable. I saw you staring at him. Did you see anything?'

Lechasseur shrugged. 'No. He wasn't a blank, exactly, like when I look at you. More the opposite, like there was far too much tied in to him for me to make head or tail of it. No lines to follow, if that makes any sense. Balls of colour mixed with darkness. Explosions and silence. I . . . had the strangest desire to touch him.'

'No kidding,' Emily said, with a little smile.

'It just felt as if it might help. He seemed on to it, though.'

After a few beats of silence, during which Emily rose and wandered to the windows, she asked: 'So what are we going to do about it?'

'I don't know,' Lechasseur said, fingering the thick envelope.

'You don't know?' Emily said, raising her eyebrows at him. 'You can't let it go! He's paid you!'

'I could return the money,' Lechasseur said plainly. Now that Crest had gone, his natural trepidation was kicking in. There'd be time travel in this somewhere, he was sure of it. What he wasn't sure of, was if he was ready for that experience again.

'You *know* there's something about him! You couldn't control yourself!' she objected. 'How could you turn your back?'

'All right, all right. We could check out his concerns a bit, I suppose,' Lechasseur shrugged, reaching for the newspaper. 'Since you seem to know more about him than I do, and, as you say, I'm having trouble controlling myself around him, maybe you can follow Crest, see what you can find out about his habits and haunts. But keep your distance, and don't do anything rash.'

'Rash? Me?' Emily smiled as she reached for the curtains. 'What are you going to do?'

'See what I can find out about the attacks,' Lechasseur said, glancing at the paper. 'Maybe these sub-humans are after him to join a beauty pageant.'

She pulled open the curtains again, and the harsh light passed through the dirt-speckled glass. The joke caught in Lechasseur's throat, for the light had illuminated the sub-heading of the article, which briefly explained how one victim of the attack, though alive, had apparently been covered in bite marks.

CHAPTER 3

Though the utter lack of a personal history had become somewhat bearable, one thing about amnesia that Emily still hadn't grown used to at all was the way it gave her a strange, often unexpected set of sympathies. Intellectually she was baffled and more than a little annoyed by the cryptic Randolph Crest, but emotionally she felt terribly sorry for him. Moreover, her pity was based not at all on his gangly, amphibious appearance, but on what she sensed as his tortured mind. She readily understood what it was like to feel out of place and often at odds with the information in one's own head.

On the other hand, not all the sympathy or empathy in the world would have prevented her from doggedly catching up with him. The aura, the weird atmosphere, the *je ne sais quoi* radiating from him had nearly as powerful an effect on Emily in memory as it had when she had faced him in the flat. Crest had struck both her and Lechasseur like a slap in the face, and she wasn't about to let that much of a mystery simply vanish. More than that, she was pleased that Lechasseur seemed to be trusting her more of late. His respect had grown, and the fact that he thought nothing of sending her out to gather information, made her feel oddly warm.

Despite some minor trepidation, Emily not only found she enjoyed being out and about, but quickly realised that the easiest way to 'tail' her target, as the Americans might say, was to walk in the brightest sunlight available. Belying the agility he had displayed in his defensive feints back at the flat, Randolph Crest moved quite slowly, doing his best to keep to the darkest of shadows.

Bell-sleeved duffle jackets were all the rage among the well-dressed women of the city, topped by small hats with large feathers. Of far lesser means, and never a slave to fashion, at least as far as she could recall, Emily had to content herself with a simple skirt and blouse. The outfit was actually to her benefit in the current circumstances, since it helped her to fade into the crowd.

Not that Crest was ogling anyone as he walked. Mostly, he stared at the ground, craning his neck forward a little in order to see past his belly. With no change in stance, he wobbled from shadow to shadow, sometimes standing stock-still for long minutes at a time, waiting until the next umbra darkened to his satisfaction.

He travelled many streets in this manner, twitching his large head left then right, eyes darting about nervously, speaking to no-one. Eventually he entered Spitalfields. As the walk progressed, it became less and less pleasant. The wide street narrowed, and on the pavement, trapped in a smaller distance between tall buildings, the sunlight shrank, the shadows grew. The buildings changed, too, shifting from larger, comfortably familiar structures, many recently rebuilt, to a series of dingy shops and dilapidated flats looking even worse than the raw plaster walls, exposed pipes and bare floorboards of Lechasseur's home.

The fashion-conscious women on the wider streets were long gone, and the looks given Emily by some of the destitute creatures leaning in the alleyways reminded her of the leering men she had first encountered when she had arrived, no, *appeared*, in London in nothing more than a pair of pyjamas. Still, she'd expected more Bohemian or academic environs for Mr Crest, and was a little surprised to realise that there wasn't a bookstore or café in sight. What's more, rather than heading toward the site of the V1 blast and the sub-human sightings, which might lend some credibility to his fears, they were moving further and further away from it.

Undeterred, though the neighbourhood grew seamier still, she followed, but soon found herself with no sunlight at all to stand in. Like Crest, she took to the shadows and tried to remain unseen.

After walking down a particularly thin, lowly street, the name of which Emily couldn't make out through the grime, Crest approached someone leaning against a building. This was a bear of a man, thick in the shoulders, a few days' growth of beard on his face. They made an odd pair, he a full head taller than Crest. She couldn't imagine what they might have in common. Emily got as close as she dared without being seen, and tried to listen, but there seemed to be little more than grunts passing between them.

In short order, the conversation murmured into silence, making the rush of passing cars a few streets away the loudest sound that came to her ears. Physical contact was broken as well. The bear man resumed his slouch against the building and looked off into the distance. Crest returned to his wobbling walk.

After a few paces, Crest turned onto an old flight of concrete steps that led down to the basement of a tall building, and soon ambled out of sight. Emily assumed he was visiting a shop, too small for her to enter unnoticed. She waited, as patiently as she could, but soon found herself edging closer and closer, hiding behind a wall, and ultimately nestling in the shadow of a particularly rank pile of old rubbish. Though the stench wrinkled her nose and threatened to make her cough, the position afforded a glimpse down the ramshackle steps, where she saw the top of a windowless door, thick with many coats of black paint. The wall beside it had no sign or number to indicated its purpose. In fact, she couldn't imagine it was anything other than some sort of storage space. But that didn't make sense. Crest had been inside now for fifteen minutes at least.

This, then, she realised, still not quite believing it, was his home. How strange. The piece she'd read about him in the papers had indicated, as far as she recalled, that he was fairly well off, as poets went. She couldn't imagine anyone inhabiting this godforsaken street of the city by choice. Still, there he was, and here she was.

Uncertain now what to do, Emily turned back in the direction of the bear man. She considered approaching him with a question or two, perhaps pretending to be a fan of Crest's work. On second look, though, she doubted the fellow had a clue that Crest was a poet. So she stood there, half-hidden by a pile of refuse, wondering what to do. She didn't want to go back to Lechasseur empty-handed.

But time wore her down. The remaining sun sank below the tops of the buildings, and the first true hints of night appeared. She was about to start the long walk home when she saw Crest's head emerge from the staircase like a black moon rising along the cracked pavement horizon. Emily stepped further back into her hiding place and tried not to inhale.

Back on the street, Crest shared a few more audible grunts with the bear man, then wobbled off into the gathering dark. This gave her some hope. Perhaps if the bear man left, she might be able to sneak into Crest's flat.

She had no such luck, however. In the next half an hour, he moved only once, to lean further back against the damaged wall, as if ready and able to melt into the immobile brick and mortar. So, finally, she decided she'd have to do nothing, or speak to him; and doing nothing was never really an option. Adding to the olfactory delights of the evening, no sooner was she clear of the smell of rubbish than she caught her first sniff of heavy spirits, an odour that grew geometrically with each step she took.

A yard or so away from the man now, trying not to let her disgust show, she forced a smile to her lips, pointed toward the staircase and said: 'Wasn't that Randolph Crest, the poet?'

The only part of the man that moved was his eyes. They shifted up just a bit to meet her own. They were so blue and bloodshot, she could see both attributes clearly, even in the near dark.

He said nothing, so she stood there and smiled until she felt so stupid doing so, that she dropped the grin and again pointed at the door.

'Randolph Crest?'

The man's fat lips parted, and he warbled. Phlegmy sounds rolled from his throat, mumbles, coughs, near words, the sense of which, if sense they had, was utterly lost on her. The gesture he made with his hand, however, was not. She hadn't even realised he'd raised his stubby fingers until she saw them, a few inches from her face, thumb rubbing index and forefinger, making a hissing sound that she thought quite loud.

She took out a coin, one of the few to her name, and handed it to him. The man took it, stuffed his hand into an unseen pocket, then lifted himself from the wall and walked off. Emily felt a rush of accomplishment, as though she'd just bought off one of the guards to an ancient tomb.

Once she was certain she was alone, she headed down the crumbling cement of the staircase, nearly tripping twice before she came to the black wooden door. The wood was rotting, frayed at the top and bottom, and it would have been a simple matter to kick it in, or even just push it off its hinges. Instead, she withdrew a hairpin, and, as Lechasseur had once shown her, used it to pick the simple lock.

A wall of stale warmth, mixed with the smell of sickly sweet sweat, pressed into her face and shoulders as she stepped into the pitch black. Papers rustled underfoot and, heart racing, she fumbled inside her skirt pocket for the electric torch she'd brought. A flick of the switch, and a sickly yellow beam shed some vague light upon the scene.

She had been right about the small, single room being intended for storage. There were no windows at all, and only one vent to the street, intended to draw off moisture, a task at which it failed abysmally. In the centre stood a familiar type of coin-operated coal stove for the winter months, though she couldn't imagine it was ever truly cold here. In one corner, there was a bed that more closely resembled the nest of a large bird. In another, a desk, and a table with a wash basin on it.

But the most striking thing about the place was that everywhere, covering everything, in pads, books, sheets and torn pieces, was paper, almost all of it covered with nervous, jagged handwriting. It was impossible to move without stepping on some of it; though there was so much, in such a state of disarray, that Emily felt sure she could have kicked a pile of it about without Crest ever being the wiser.

She made her way over to the desk and pulled some of the fresher-looking sheets into the torch light. Most were letters to and from other poets and academics, some about Crest's work, others sharing his thoughts on theirs. Nearly every one of Crest's began with an apology for never meeting his correspondent in person, and an assurance that he held their friendship no less dear for lack of physical contact. From what Emily could make out, Crest had no friends that he'd ever actually met.

There was a set of more formal letters from a Mr Alan Bungard, inviting Crest to give a recitation of some of his works in public at a small venue in London. Oddly, though Crest had clearly hesitated for many months, under Bungard's gentle pressure, he had eventually acquiesced.

There were many more items that Emily perused. A number were pieces of Crest's poetry, some new, some appearing very old. A verse or two caught Emily's eye:

That it cannot speak, I know
but have to wonder if such muteness
Is born of deficiency,
Or if its language, unknown to me,
Speaks of higher plains

And the oddly erotic:

Dark opens in wider circles
Trickling down my sides
Kissing my animal body so tightly
With her tongue
I breathe alive another day

And so on. Never much for poetry, Emily had no idea whether they were any good, but she didn't think it the sort of thing she would read on her own. Having quickly had her fill of Crest's homages to night and lightlessness, she turned the torch to the rest of the room, hoping to make some sense out of the clutter.

It was then that a particularly large, unwieldy pile of paper caught her eye, mostly because it was stacked far higher than the natural chaos of the rest of the room would permit. He'd obviously piled it all there on purpose. But why? To protect something? To bury something? Briefly worried that she might find the skull of a literary critic, she steeled herself for a closer look.

The top and middle sections of the paper tower seemed haphazard enough, but at the bottom, beneath a pile of crumpled pages and torn paper scraps, some of which contained no more than the first few letters of an unfinished word, she saw a singular book. The light brown edge of the leather cover glowed from the bottom of the pile. It was thick, expensively bound, but very worn.

Crossing her fingers, she used her foot to shovel a few bits of detritus delicately to either side of the book, then kneeled and gently pulled it out. To her delight, the tower remained intact.

With a shiver, despite the heat, she flipped through the first few pages, and soon realised that she held a diary. Later entries contained rough notes for Crest's poems, but the further back she went, the more child-like the handwriting became, until finally it decayed into a series of unrecognisable symbols. She was just about to begin reading what she could in earnest, when the door creaked and began to open.

The master of the house had returned.

CHAPTER 4

At about the same time, Honoré Lechasseur, now somewhere between Green Park and Hyde Park Corner, straddled his bicycle and eyed the police-guarded entrance to the abandoned, and now partly destroyed, Constitution Hill station. There were three bobbies outside, doubtless more within. He figured it was more a show of force to calm the public than a strategic decision. It was apparent from the newspaper article that there were many other ways in and out – otherwise the attacks would have been stopped easily. As it was, with miles and miles of tube tunnel interconnecting all London, the Subterraneans, as the papers had dubbed them, were free to surface anywhere.

The bigger question was whether or not these creatures had any connection at all with Randolph Crest, beyond the crazed poet's imagination. Lechasseur had hoped that if he surveyed the scene of the blast and the locales of the attacks, his time sensitivity might react to something, perhaps even in the same way it'd reacted to Crest himself. So far, there had been nothing, and he'd taken to staring at the bobbies, hoping one of them might have been inside at some point.

Even this proved fruitless. His powers, still dizzying, were also still hopelessly beyond his control. The only thing he'd been able to see were the fried eggs and tomato that the man had enjoyed for breakfast. It was clear that Lechasseur wasn't going to be able to get inside the blast area, either via the obvious entrance or via his own, more subtle and indirect means.

Finally, one of the officers, in between regularly shifting his weight from the heels to the balls of his feet, took notice of Lechasseur and furrowed his brow warily. Lechasseur managed a slight grin, tipped his hat in greeting, then rode off, rattling off the facts in his mind as he pedalled.

That the V1 explosion had somehow 'awoken' or 'freed' these creatures from somewhere underground was never in doubt – the timing coincided completely. There was either a family of four or five of the creatures, or that was the size of one of their hunting packs. At night, they came out from the tube tunnels or the sewers, or whatever other dark underground places were available, found food, living or otherwise, then went back to wherever home was.

Though their sorties could hardly be described as peaceful, the creatures generally seemed less involved with cannibalism and more interested in acquiring more socially acceptable sorts of food, particularly sweets. Most of the sightings had taken place near food shops and restaurants, anywhere that something edible could be found. The worst damage that had been done was to a sweet shop, which, in the space of a half hour, had been completely stripped of its wares. The hapless owner, who'd been present unpacking stock, was hospitalised with a chunk of his thigh missing.

The descriptions made these foraging attackers out to be humanoid, though somewhat shorter and far more muscular than men, but their behaviour was completely animal. Lechasseur found himself comforted by their beastliness. Animals were predictable, understandable. They ate when hungry, and attacked usually only when backed into a corner. Humans, on the other hand, particularly those like Crest, were not only unpredictable, they were capable of the most insane cruelty. He'd seen enough of that during the War.

Slowly, pretending leisure, he rode around the block. He was out of sight of the police now, scanning the alleys and gutters for anything unusual. A glint of something silver on the ground caught his eye in the dim glow of a street-lamp. He almost thought nothing of it, but with little else to do, he dismounted from the bike and went down on his knees for a closer look. It was the foil and torn paper from a chocolate bar wrapper, half-wedged in a sewer cover. Nothing suspicious. Or was it?

Recalling the Subterraneans' affinity for sweets, Lechasseur idly pulled at the wrapper. It came free with a tug. Though the light was dim, it was obvious that the tears in the foil and paper had been caused by chewing, as if a dog had been given the bar fully wrapped and hadn't quite been able to distinguish between the covering and the contents.

Lechasseur stood and looked around. The sewer cover was opposite an alley behind the blast site. Wheeling his bicycle alongside him, he went into the alley and, after a few yards, spotted the remains of another, similarly mauled chocolate bar. Further down, there was another. The alley ended in a brick wall, too sheer and high to climb, and with no visible entrance. With nowhere else to go, he walked back to the street, stood in the pool of light beneath the street-lamp and took a closer look at his prized detritus. The wrappers were shredded, nearly eaten themselves, with not a drop of chocolate remaining.

He lifted one to his face and sniffed, immediately wrinkling his nose. There was saliva, sharp and unsavoury, still on the wrapper. It was recent. Either the creatures had already returned from their nightly raid, which was unlikely, or they'd just gone out.

After chaining his bike to the lamppost, Lechasseur sighed and went over to the manhole cover. Part of him prayed he wouldn't be able to get it open, but the cover came free with a tug. The smell from the wrapper had been bad enough, but the stench of waste from the sewers made his head swim. It brought to mind a newspaper piece that Emily had read to him once about London's early problems with sewage. In 1858, the 'Great Stink' from a backed-up Thames, had caused thousands to flee the city. At that moment, as he climbed down into the smell, Lechasseur knew just how they'd felt.

He had no idea what he was going to do once he was down there, other than perhaps be sick. As it turned out, the concrete walkway at the bottom of the ladder was moist, but not submerged. After a few minutes, his eyes could make out some of his surroundings, mostly thanks to the weak light that filtered down from the regularly-placed grates and manhole covers above.

It was this light that revealed another wrapper, floating in the muck. Five yards later there was another, clinging to a mossy wall. Before he knew it, Lechasseur had followed the haphazard trail a hundred yards through what seemed more a bad dream than a physical place. Then, abruptly, the trail of wrappers ceased.

He stood there a moment, hoping that wherever Emily was, it smelt better than this, and wondering what to do next. The creatures were not here; or, if they were, they made no sound. Given that even his softest steps echoed endlessly, he doubted that anything living could move down here without making a noise. Why, then, had the trail gone cold?

They must have surfaced, he reasoned, briefly thinking of them as a U-boat. Looking up, he realised that he stood directly beneath another manhole cover. He berated himself for not seeing it sooner, but the smell, he realised, had made his head even fuzzier than usual.

Straining with the effort, Lechasseur shifted the heavy circle of metal. With a loud grating noise, it lifted up and slid to one side. Lechasseur poked his head up out of the hole and found it opened onto a quiet street. There, on the ground, a few yards away, was another chewed wrapper. Beyond that was a small garden square, nestled between the walls of three two-storey buildings, with a large, white stone fountain in the centre. To the right of the park, a well-dressed man was trying to comfort a slender woman.

The woman was screaming hysterically.

Lechasseur clambered out of the sewer. His sudden appearance caused the couple to turn and face him, which only made the woman scream more. Lechasseur held his hands out, to try to indicate that he was not a threat, and stepped quickly into the light near the gate. It was then that he noticed a shadow moving swiftly among the bushes in the park. Something had been hiding there, and, with Lechasseur about to block the park's only exit, had now decided it was time to leave. It rose and skittered, half on the ground, half along the iron fence. By the time the couple saw the expression on Lechasseur's face and looked toward where he was looking, it was somewhere else.

Lechasseur could still see it, though. It raced along the wall of one of the buildings that bordered three sides of the park, using invisible finger holds, four feet up. Then it hit the ground again, leapt, rolled, and dived for the far wall, all the while moving closer to the exit where Lechasseur stood, dumfounded.

With no more than two yards between them, the shadow bounded off one of the concrete posts of the gate, directly towards Lechasseur. He braced himself, prepared to be knocked off his feet. Instead, he felt a heavy paw, or hand, press against his shoulder for leverage. The thing shot over and above him, then clambered off into the street. As far as Lechasseur could make out, it looked like a combination between a chimp and a fast-moving lizard.

As it made its way toward the open sewer, Lechasseur realised it was not alone. Two or three others, moving so quickly, camouflaged so well, that he hadn't noticed them at all, slipped down into the sewer along with it. He felt a sudden relief that he'd not run into them down there in the dark.

Unwilling to follow without a weapon, and perhaps a small army, Lechasseur turned back towards the fountain and the terrified couple. The woman's screams had muffled into sobs. A growing police siren wailed in the distance, but underlying it all was the bubbling of the fountain, which Lechasseur saw clearly now. Its pulsing water was dark red.

A hand jutted from the surface, the wet sleeve of a coat clinging to the skin. Its lifeless fingers were stretched out, as if to try to grasp onto the last moments of life.

Lechasseur realised that this attack was not quite like the others. There was no obvious food to be had here, and the victim had been drowned, on purpose.

Maybe, Lechasseur reasoned sadly, *these things are more human than I thought.*

CHAPTER 5

The next night, half an hour after an eggy orange sun plopped below the smoggy grey cityscape, Mr Jerome Windleby of 14 Bath Court leaned forward across his makeshift dining room table and deeply inhaled the wafting aroma of his freshly-cooked, hard-won cut of prime beef.

Heat from the kitchen pressed uncomfortably against his wide back, raising some sweat beneath his white, button-down shirt, but a cooler breeze from the open windows, just across from the crate at which he sat, hit his face and mixed quite pleasantly with the smell of his first steak dinner in years.

Half in hell, half in heaven, Windleby mused, delighted to be half anywhere and very pleased that, in the end, his cooking skills had turned out to be not quite so bad as his late wife had believed. As he'd guessed, procuring the meat had been much harder than preparing it. Usually, he sold his meat ration tickets to cover more immediate bills, but over the last few weeks, he'd had a good streak at the impromptu book stall that he ran along the iron railings of Green Park on Piccadilly, and had even sold a rare hardback edition of *Tarzan of the Apes*, signed by Burroughs, for a few pounds.

After staring for hours at the extra money, as though it was a little green man from Mars, or, perhaps more accurately, a lamp-locked genie, he'd decided to treat himself to a slap-up steak dinner, followed by apple pie and custard. That was when the hard part had begun. Despite running a book stall, he had no knack for bargaining. His little pencilled-in prices on the inside covers were not negotiable. The world of spivs and black market goods, however, was based on a nearly Middle-Eastern system of haggling. Simply to pay the asking price was practically to invite tainted goods. One had to show strength, knowledge and intuition. Mr Windleby had none of these, and upon meeting his first spiv, he'd mumbled a few words, coughed, then run off.

By and by, the desire for a good meal had driven him back, and he'd hemmed and hawed his way into the prize that now lay before him – mostly by pretending to be a man of more means than he was, and promising repeat business. He was quite certain he'd still paid too much for it, but the fact that the meat smelled fresh made him quite proud.

He'd thought briefly of reading the paper with dinner, as he'd done before Doris had been killed during the Blitz. He'd hoped that returning to such an old habit might bring to mind the sound of her reprimanding 'tch' – which, in life, had always made him lay the paper down to talk with her. But, seeing as how there could no longer be any such conversation, coupled with the fact that the paper was full of the dreadful death of Mr Lemuel Waterman, who had been bludgeoned and drowned in a fountain by a gang of hairy ruffians that some claimed were underground monsters, he decided to forego the trip down memory lane and concentrate fully on his hard-earned meal.

He rubbed his hands together boyishly, then filled them with cutlery. Reaching forward, steak knife in one hand, fork in the other, he noticed for the first time that the hairs on the back of his hand had started to turn white. Funny, he still remembered himself as young. Now why would memory lie about a simple thing like that? With a nod to whatever gods happened to be looking in, he raised the piece of dripping meat to his mouth, and hoped memory hadn't lied about the taste of a good steak.

The succulent morsel was just about to touch his tongue when a scraping sound from the hall made him close his mouth and turn.

The sound came again, louder, closer to the door.

A dog?

Not bloody likely. Windleby lived at the top of a four storey building. The only flat here was his. The only way up was via a long flight of steps. Not the sort of trek one would accidentally make with a pooch.

But then the sounds came again.

Squirrels?

Perhaps some of the little buggers had made their way down from the roof. Sometimes as he lay awake at night, he could hear them skittering about, looking for nuts, nesting in the attic, or simply falling, having misjudged the distance to one of the tree branches that overhung the building. Still, the furry interlopers tended to be an autumn or winter occurrence. In the high summer, they kept to the outdoors.

The sound came again. It was now nearly right behind the door. More than that, in the distance, he thought he could hear someone quickly climbing the steps. He briefly considered putting down his food-laden fork and going to have a look, but in a rare burst of self-esteem, decided: *No, I'm going to eat my dinner!*

With that, he stuffed the forkful into his mouth, bit deeply and let the juices wash about his tongue. His eyes rolled into his head. He let himself gurgle with pleasure.

The scraping, distant though it now seemed in his mind, was actually beginning to make the door shake a bit. Windleby had just managed to stuff a second, larger bite into his mouth, when it splintered.

Still chewing, saddened at the thought of leaving his tiny bliss behind so quickly, he turned just in time to see three figures careening madly into his humble home, knocking over what minor furnishings he still possessed and tearing his few pictures from the wall as they amazingly climbed along its sheer surface.

He wished they had been dogs. Had they more hair, he might have thought them apes. Had they less, he might have thought them human. As it was, there was little he could think as they threw themselves at him, sending the lit candles and his plate flying.

He felt a rapid heartbeat (his own?) and smelled foetid breath as he tumbled backwards onto the floor. Hands (and feet?) tore at him, fumbling for a hold on his old muscles and flesh.

'Help, help . . .' he said, quite softly, unwilling to truly believe this was taking place, tonight of all nights. When, though, they began dragging him across the floor, not towards the door, but towards the open window, a voice deep down inside him, that sounded remarkably like that of his deceased wife, insisted he would be wise to raise his voice as much as his aging throat and lungs allowed. Unable to disagree, he screamed at the top of his lungs.

'HELP! HELP! THEY'RE KILLING ME!'

As if the shouting didn't hurt enough on its own, a greasy hand wedged itself into his wide-open mouth, briefly stifling his cries. Gagging at the horrible taste of oil, salt and an odd sweetness, Windleby bit down as hard as he could, cutting flesh and drawing blood. Accompanied by the sound of a fierce, bird-like yelp, the hand withdrew. Windleby was free to begin screaming anew, which he did. Unfortunately, he was almost to the window.

As he realised he would likely die, his chest began to hurt. A pounding filled his ears that he thought was that of his over-burdened heart. It turned out, instead, to be the heavy steps of someone storming into the room. Twisting his head, opening his eyes, he saw, though the image was a bit blurred, a tall Negro in a black leather trench coat and fedora. The fellow rushed in, swinging a piece of what looked like Doris's favourite end table over his head.

There was a sound of splintering wood, some barks, some human shouts; and, at some point, a second person, a young woman with long, dark hair, had also entered the flat. Of more importance to Windleby, the creatures that held him let go, leaving him to cough, sputter and roll in pain on the floor. Seconds later, he heard the sound of breaking glass. The creatures were exiting, not through the door, but through the window.

By the time the young woman switched on a lamp, Windleby was wheezing and terrified, but otherwise healthy. He watched her scan the wreckage of the flat, which mere minutes ago had been perfectly neat, and heard her say to the Negro, who was out of sight behind him: 'Not exactly random foraging, was it?'

'For certain,' the man replied, still breathless himself. 'They targeted this place. Headed straight for it from the same spot I saw them at last night. But these last two attacks just don't fit at all with the pattern reported in the papers. It's almost as though they're working to some plan now.'

'But how?' the woman said, as she walked over to Windleby's shivering form. 'From what I could see and sense, they don't seem to have the ability to speak.'

'An animal trainer then?' the man asked.

Windleby felt her hand wiping his hair from his eyes, improving his view. Her touch calmed him a bit.

She looked Windleby in the eyes and said, warmly: 'Looks like you'll be all right. Just to be sure, though, we should see about getting you to a doctor.'

'W-who . . . are you?' Windleby said, weakly.

'And what's the connection to Crest?' the man asked, more to himself than to anyone present.

'Maybe none, but I can't help but feel there's a link,' said the woman. 'A strong one.'

'Who are you?' Windleby repeated hoarsely. But he couldn't be sure they heard him at all.

'Me, too,' the man said. 'Of course, your recent encounter with him makes it a little awkward for us to ask him.'

Taking his observation as a reproach, she stiffened and turned towards her friend. 'It wasn't my fault, you know. I don't have a lot of experience with tailing people, at least as far as I know. And he hasn't fired us, not officially.'

'I know, I know. I just never expected you'd break into his home. I asked you not to do anything dangerous.'

'Well, too late for that. It was already dangerous.'

'Why? What was he going to do while you followed him? Sweat on you?'

'I don't think *that's* fair! That was a horrible neighbourhood, full of recently-released convicts and alcoholics!'

'Right. Sorry.'

'I insist,' Windleby interrupted, beginning to recover more fully, as he propped himself up on his elbows, 'that you both tell me immediately, who you are!'

Suddenly hearing, the man pushed air between his lips apologetically and answered: 'Sorry, sir. I'm Honoré Lechasseur . . . I . . . '

Recognising the name, Windleby's face turned red as he saw the Negro clearly for the first time. 'You're that spiv! I told you, sir, that I did not want your meat and had made other arrangements! What kind of petty creature are you to have your ruffians attack me in my home?'

'What?' Lechasseur said, shocked. But then Windleby's face jogged a small memory, so his protests were tinged with a sort of sputtering confusion. Emily suppressed a giggle.

'I'm . . . we're . . . not with them!' Lechasseur said. 'We came here to save your life, sir!'

A light rustling came from outside the window; nothing more, perhaps, than the wind moving through the trees. Ignoring it, Windleby pushed himself to his feet, adjusted his shirt and barked: 'Sir, I believe that's a matter for the police to sort out!'

The mention of the police did little to calm Lechasseur. 'Do what you like, of course, but let me point out that you're quite lucky we got here when we did! Those . . . things don't scare easy!'

The rustling came again. This time, Emily cast a glance towards the broken lattice work.

'Nor do I, sir,' Windleby said. Having felt so helpless ten minutes ago, embracing his sense of outrage gave him a sense of strength.

Unfortunately, at that moment, he saw, from the corner of his eye, the creatures returning, in force. Like large, humanoid insects, they swarmed in from the night. Three . . . five . . . seven and more, pushing in, crawling along the walls, floor and ceiling. Windleby saw Lechasseur and Emily trying to reach him, but they were pushed back by sheer dint of numbers.

Hands and feet again surrounded him, and this time there were oh so many more. This time, they did not drag, but lifted. His felt his back sag as they hoisted him, his old vertebrae cracking into and out of place from the hitherto unexperienced position. He saw the high ceiling of his flat grow closer, then move as they carried him along. He felt splintered wood scratch at his sides as they took him out through the window.

The smell, the breathing, the clawing was more, Windleby thought, than he could possibly bear. As he flailed helplessly against his attackers, he found himself nearly in tears, wondering why the cosmos had been so cruel as to not allow him the small comfort of the fine meal he'd prepared for himself.

Then, all of a sudden, as if in answer to his pleas, he was freed of their suffocating embrace forever. The very last thing Windleby saw was the inlaid brick floor of the courtyard in front of his building, rushing up with the full force of the earth to meet his frail human form.

CHAPTER 6

Mid-morning the next day, as Emily padded across the bare floor of his flat, Lechasseur tried to get a glimpse of the wounds under her clothing. From what he could tell, the blood had already dried into long, thin protective scabs along the scratches on her body. He watched, feeling her foul mood, as she stepped over to the curtains and yanked them open. He dared not make a sound when the dark, rainy cityscape was revealed, but her expression indicated she knew exactly what he was thinking.

Still exhausted from the previous evening's events, he was sprawled in his easy chair, rubbing the central knot of a huge, white and blue bruise on his left forearm. It had swollen considerably while he slept. Cautiously, he stretched his arm out and winced. Nothing broken. If he worked it a bit, he might even get some use out of it by the end of the day.

Emily leaned her shoulder between two holes in the white plaster wall and looked out grimly at the steady rain. Now it was Lechasseur's turn to believe he knew her thoughts.

'Come on,' he said, trying to sound soothing. 'You gave them a few good kicks in the shins. I saw one of them skittering off in pain before the others pinned you.'

'It didn't help Mr Windleby,' she answered numbly.

Lechasseur shrugged. 'Neither did I. But there must have been fifty of those things. We would have needed an army.'

She turned to face him. 'I know. I just can't help but think that if we'd got him out sooner, or done something different . . . '

'You'll drive yourself crazy like that,' Lechasseur said.

'No,' she said, a little angrily. 'Other people drive themselves mad with maybes and might-have-beens, but *we* can change things!'

Part of him agreed with her, but he didn't want to admit it. He didn't at all care for his proximity to death over the last few days. The sight of two bodies, both mangled and bleeding, had stirred a deep, wounded sickness inside him, bringing brighter hues and louder screams to the stray flashbacks that haunted his dreams. No less disconcerting was his brief fear, during the attack, that Emily had been killed, too. He'd feared that once before, even seen her dead body thanks to a strange twist in the time trails.

The more time passed, the more he grew attached to her. It seemed to have something to do with their twinned abilities, as if they were bonding inextricably. The relief he'd felt when he'd found her rolled up in a ball in a corner of Windleby's room, bleeding but alive, had been akin to the sensation he'd once felt when a grenade had gone off a few feet from him, and, after he'd staggered to his feet, he'd realised with infinite pleasure that he still had both his arms.

But the knot of his feelings, and their potential to change the path of time, were not things he was willing to deal with at the moment.

'Right now we can barely stand,' he offered instead. 'And who knows what to change, anyway?'

Emily poked herself in the chest. 'We should. We should know.'

'To tell the truth,' he answered, 'I don't even know why we survived. Why didn't they kill us?'

'Don't know,' Emily answered. The issue seemed to distract her, engage a different part of her mind. 'But you're right. They seemed so intent on their mission that they practically ignored us once we were out of the way. And what are they? I mean, they're definitely humanoid, but they seem to have such a strong pack mentality, more than any apes I've seen, and certainly more than people. It was like they were of one mind.'

Lechasseur waved the hand of his good, right arm at the newspaper in his lap. 'Paper calls them troglodytes, primitive humans, cavemen. They've got the looks to fit the bill, but they certainly haven't been acting that way the last two nights.'

'Do you think perhaps they're aliens or mutants or something?' Emily wondered.

'Creatures from another world?' A few weeks ago that idea would have seemed absurd, but not now. Even so, he didn't consider it likely. 'No. I think maybe they were human once, like us, but got stuck under London somehow, and . . . adapted.' Lechasseur spoke with vague conviction as he pulled the newspaper up along his chest for a closer look. 'Without the light, maybe their other senses grew stronger, like this pack mentality thing.'

'Not a very pretty adaptation, is it?' Emily said.

'Well . . . who knows what they look like to each other? Besides, it's not really about aesthetics, is it? It's about survival. And at the moment, the score seems to be in their favour.'

Emily looked at him scornfully. 'Well, I hope it's at least a *little* about aesthetics,' she said. 'It can't just be about who eats whom!'

'Speaking of eating, I noticed something back at Windleby's flat,' Lechasseur said.

'What?'

'Apple pie sitting in the kitchen. Ripped to shreds.'

'So?'

'So, whatever was keeping them from nibbling on us wasn't strong enough to keep them from the sugar. I mean, I followed a trail of half-eaten wrappers! Their natural instincts aren't being completely suppressed. But add it all together and we still haven't got much. Two dead, perhaps intentionally assassinated, and a client who won't speak to us.'

Emily smiled at that. 'Well, we have a chance to make it up to Crest. He's doing a public reading of his poetry tonight, at a small hall off Tottenham Court Road.'

'Really?' Lechasseur was genuinely surprised. 'He didn't strike me as much of a publicity hound.'

'He's not, but in the letters I read, the gentleman who runs the show, Alan Bungard, managed to appeal to his ego quite effectively. I think we should go.'

Lechasseur nodded, then added: 'And I'll try to keep my hands off him.' He tossed her the paper. 'I'm tired, aching and not at all happy,' he said. 'Probably a little blind right now, too. Maybe you can get something out of this.'

He watched her take the folded paper and start to skim the central articles. Satisfied that she'd be busy for a bit, he turned to examine the rest of his own wounds. His long leather coat had saved him from some of the deep scratches that Emily had received, but his desperate efforts to reach Windleby had also made him more of a target.

After a long silence, he said: 'Anything?'

She shrugged. 'Nothing really. Just the names.'

Lechasseur waved a hand, indicating that she should continue.

'Mr Waterman was drowned in a fountain. Mr Windleby died from a fall. Water and wind. There's this parallel between their names and the way they died,' she said. 'As if *that's* why they were chosen.'

'But what . . . ' Lechasseur began. Then it dawned on him. 'As if for a sacrifice? Some sort of ritual? That would fit in with the idea of an outside force controlling them. These little devils don't have the capacity for ritual magic, but someone else might.' Excited now, Lechasseur stood up and joined her by the window. 'Anything else about the victims?' he asked, his mind beginning to race.

'No,' she said.

'Obituaries. Check the obituaries. Waterman will have been in yesterday's paper.' He headed for a small table in the kitchen area. It was there that he left the old newspapers in a huge, disorganised pile. 'Let's look for something that might make him a suitable sacrifice; a significant date of birth or lineage or something like that.'

As Lechasseur sifted through the pile, Emily reported: 'Windleby was born 27 January 1889. That would make him . . . an Aquarius.'

'You know your hokum, eh? But no luck with the theory, then. Aquarius is a water sign, isn't it?'

Emily shook her head. 'No. It's the water-bearer, but it's a fixed air sign.'

Lechasseur, having just located the previous day's paper, looked up at her sharply. 'Are you sure? Did you study this somewhere?'

'Not that I know of. But it's all right here on the opposite page, in the horoscopes. There are three signs for each element: earth, air, fire and water. Each is either mutable, cardinal or fixed. Fixed, I guess, is the airiest of the air signs.'

'Okay then, what's the fixed water sign?' asked Lechasseur, searching through his own paper.

'Scorpio,' she read. '23 October to 21 November.'

'Bingo,' Lechasseur said. 'Mr Waterman was born on 30 October.' Excited, he looked across at Emily, hoping she would come up with what they should do next.

Two hours later, she did.

When they reached the foot of the flight of old stone steps leading up to the imposing main entrance of Somerset House, Lechasseur stopped cold, sighed audibly and rolled his eyes. 'Come on, don't you think this is just a little silly?'

By the time he'd finished his sentence, Emily was ten steps ahead. Seeing he was no longer right behind her, she sighed herself, stopped, turned, ran back down, then began yanking him after her by the sleeve of his trench coat. A few passers-by stopped to stare at the light young girl pulling the taller, stronger black man. Despite the rain, she was wearing only a white blouse and skirt. Next to Lechasseur's black coat, she stood out like a beacon.

'We've come this far, and neither of us has had any better ideas,' she insisted. 'Besides, we've only a few hours before Crest's reading. Wouldn't want to get bad seats.'

'A few *hours*? *Here*?' Lechasseur said in a pained tone. Then he gave in, pulled his arm back and trotted alongside her up the steps to the public records office.

After twenty minutes of being politely bandied about from one confused clerk to another, they were finally taken to a small room stacked with files. There, they were introduced to a long, lean, white haired man whose glasses made his eyes seem the size of small, black plums. He, the others assured him, would at least be able to understand the question.

Taking turns, the duo explained as best they could.

When the man didn't say anything for several minutes, Emily felt nonetheless obligated to ask again: 'We'd like a list of people currently residing in London who were born between 21 April and 21 May and whose surnames somehow relate to earth, and a list of people born between 23 July and 21 August whose surnames somehow relate to fire.'

The plum-eyed clerk turned to Lechasseur, who grinned sheepishly.

'And you would like this information as well?' the clerk said.

'Yes, please,' Lechasseur answered.

'Well, let's see,' the clerk began, superciliously. 'The last time we counted, back in 1939, there were about eight and a half million people in London. Of course, that's a bit dated, but they cancelled the last census due to the War, so let's say, for the sake of an easy calculation, that there are currently about eight million people living in the city.'

He paused to let that information sink in, then continued, raising a single finger for each new verbal calculation that he made. 'The two time periods you gave me are roughly a month apiece. I realise this next bit isn't very scientific, since birth rates rise and fall throughout the year, giving an uneven distribution over any twelve month cycle, but if you divided that by twelve, you'd have roughly 708,000 people for each of the two periods you mentioned, making a total of 1,416,000 persons. Now, I have no idea exactly how one might determine how many of those might or might not have names associated with earth or fire, other than by reviewing each record individually.'

Emily seemed genuinely confused. 'But don't you have some sort of machine you could just type the question into and have it spit the answers out at the other end?'

Lechasseur and the clerk both looked at her.

'No, madam, we do not,' the clerk said with finality.

Emily rubbed her forehead as her face turned red. 'I'm so sorry. It just seemed to me that perhaps you should.'

She grabbed Lechasseur's coat arm and, with a sheepish glance at the clerk, started back toward the exit. The clerk stood and watched them go, a look of bemusement on his face.

CHAPTER 7

To call it a hall was something of an exaggeration. The small space, in a building just behind an old church, would have been much more suited to an intimate study group than a large public reading. But Alan Bungard, a slim, wiry man of limitless energy, with sparkling blue eyes and a pencil thin moustache not unlike Lechasseur's, had managed to squeeze in about fifty folding chairs. And they were rapidly filling up.

The crowd was eclectic; artists, literary types, students and academics who'd actually heard of Randolph Crest were mixed in with a few wealthier patrons of the arts. There were even some members of the working class present, looking for some free entertainment. Given the variety of attendees, no-one cast a second glance as Emily and Lechasseur entered.

A table near the entrance held a pile of folded programmes, each containing copies of the poems that Crest would be reading and featuring a small photograph of the author on the back cover. Though the photographer had done his best, he hadn't managed to make the man seem at all attractive.

Lechasseur grabbed a copy and showed it to Emily. 'Not the choice I'd make,' he said, sniggering a bit. 'Advertising Mr Crest's froggy face?'

'Doesn't seem to have stopped them from coming, though,' Emily said. 'This isn't a half bad crowd.'

'Gives us some place to hide, I suppose, until we're ready to speak to him.' Lechasseur pointed to two free seats in the back row, far from the podium and shielded by a wall of people.

Emily shook her head and marched towards the front. 'I think we should get it over with,' she said.

Lechasseur followed reluctantly. 'How angry did you say he was?' he asked, as they reached the front row.

Emily shrugged. 'Hard to tell, really. He's given to hysterics, then he starts jumbling his words. I'm sure he's calmed down by now.'

'Thieves! Burglars!' a high pitched voice hissed from behind a curtain near the podium. Crest's large, round head poked out from behind, his eyes bulging alarmingly. Completing his resemblance to a half-animal character from the works of Charles Dodgson, he wore a black tuxedo, his bow tie hopelessly askew.

'Here, you dare to come?' he half-whispered, unable to contain himself. The natural murmuring of the crowd was the only thing muting his cries enough to avoid attention.

Lechasseur turned back, but then froze. The powerful rush of intuition that made him want to reach out and touch this man had returned. He was caught between instincts. Emily, similarly affected, had no trouble deciding how to handle it. She rushed over to Crest, projecting, in her own low whisper, in as contrite a tone as she could muster: 'I'm so sorry, Mr Crest. Please, if you'll just allow me to explain . . .'

Though it seemed scarcely possible, Crest's eyes went wider, enhancing their toad-like qualities even more. He pulled back violently. 'Explain? Explain to the police!' he shouted hysterically. 'Explain to your God why you felt the right to trample on the pieces of my bleeding heart!'

This time, Crest did gain some attention from the crowd. Alan Bungard, his normally cheery face suddenly concerned, strode from the side of the room with surprisingly quick steps.

'I am so . . .' Emily began again, but this time, Lechasseur cut her off and spoke in a slow, steady voice.

'Mr Crest, we only thought you should know that we've found out quite a bit about the attacks,' he said. But then Bungard stepped forcibly between Crest and what he deemed the source of the problem: Lechasseur and Emily.

'Are you being disturbed, Mr Crest?' he asked, but he was looking at Lechasseur.

Closing his eyes fractionally, Crest pursed his lips and wrinkled his brow. The loose skin on his face was such that the use of those muscles created additional wrinkling near his temples, giving him quite a monstrous look. If he'd been at all otherwise imposing, he might have been frightening. As it was, the face only made him seem more comical.

'No, no problem,' he said, after a pause. 'I'm simply very excited.'

Bungard gave a little bow and withdrew.

'Afterwards, we'll speak,' Crest said to Lechasseur. 'The female can come, too, but I don't want her talking.'

Emily made a face, but Lechasseur nodded as if he understood. Crest turned back towards the dais, hesitated, then faced them again.

'And do *not* sit in the front row,' he whispered, sounding like some sort of reptile. Having no wish to offend him further, Lechasseur and Emily complied, and found themselves in the fifth row, behind some fairly large poetry aficionados who they hoped might conceal their presence entirely.

After a customary delay, Bungard made the usual opening comments about how much he appreciated the support of so and so, and how delighted he was to be able to present such a renowned poet as Mr Randolph Crest, in his first public reading since before the War. Crest's outburst had rattled the audience, and as a result, the applause was muted, possibly for fear that any loud noise might upset the highly-strung poet further.

Crest stepped out onto the podium, nodding in a practiced fashion. He looked down at the assembled crowd, but made eye contact with no-one. His face was covered with the patina of sweat familiar to Lechasseur and Emily. Shaking slightly, he stood behind the lectern and mumbled something that may have been: 'Thank you.'

As the audience wondered if his weak voice would carry to the back of the room for the duration of the reading, Crest reached into his jacket pocket and withdrew a folded copy of the programme. Shaking, he slowly unfolded it, flicked off a bit of sweat that had fallen from his brow onto the front page, then turned to the first poem. This, according to the notes, had received favourable reviews in *Anataeus* and *The Spectator*. In any event, head bent low, rising slowly up and down as if in ritual prayer, he began to read.

> *Things, such as I, decay,*
> *Time wins without raising a hand.*

At first sight of this ubiquitous dissolution,
I don't surrender so much as sigh,
Wondering why I failed to see so large so long.

The audience was silent, so not only the words, but also his rasping breaths, were perfectly audible. As he read, some of the stray twitches of his body stopped and slowed. His voice dropped in pitch just enough to be bearable, and some might say it had a slight musical lilt.

But I know, my masks suffocated my lungs,
My wickedness blurred my eyes,
So that now, a thousand darker dreams return,
Grown all the more misshapen,
By my abdication as their king.

Midway through, Crest's bearing changed notably, as if he were entering a trance. He now spoke with an eerie intimacy, as if his own words had cast a spell on him and he'd forgotten that he wasn't the only person present.

Memory steals the form I begged to inhabit.
Instead the sea-self welcomes the demons
That swarm from the centre of the world,
All cackles, eyes and teeth.
While I, a voice among the moans, am drowned.

He looked up and seemed quite surprised to see the audience again. No-one seemed to know whether to applaud or not, until Bungard clapped his hands together. Not wishing to be rude, but appearing a bit stunned, the rest of the audience joined in.

'Pretty dreary, wasn't it?' Lechasseur said, clapping politely himself.

Emily leaned over and whispered: 'Actually, that's one of the cheerier ones. At least the demons don't die in it.'

'Ah,' he answered, wondering just how long poetry readings generally lasted.

The next few poems, paeans to death and darkness with some overtures to postmodernism, Yeats and Eliot, proceeded without event.

Lechasseur even enjoyed a short bit about the Black Queen of Storms, but only because, in boredom, he'd imagined the Queen as Lena Horne, a favourite actress, and he as her welcome suitor.

'Stormy Weather' was still playing in Lechasseur's mind when Emily nudged him in the shoulder. She nodded towards Crest and whispered: 'Does he look ill to you?'

'As opposed to what?' Lechasseur answered. Then he realised that Crest had stopped speaking and was just standing there, wheezing.

The audience were beginning to whisper. Bungard had taken a few steps forward. Crest made an odd, phlegmatic noise that sounded somewhere between a cough and a bowl of custard slopping onto a table top. He was clearing his throat. Bungard stopped, but his muscles remained visibly tense.

'I'd wanted to . . .' Crest began. He wheezed again and wiped his brow with his hand. Apparently forgetting where he was, he flicked the bits of sweat from his fingertips out into the front row, making Lechasseur quite glad that he and Emily had changed their seats. Bungard took another half-step, but Crest seemed to recover.

'For this occasion . . . it's not quite finished . . . but here . . .' he said.

Audience members began turning towards one another, as if they'd missed something. But then, Crest's head turned up to the ceiling, leaving the folds of his substantial neck facing the audience. Then he began to sort of chant:

> *Four corners of the world, Four edges of the mind of God,*
> *Permitted to be seen by Man, I beseech you*
> *Open my eyes to you, and your will to this rough beast.*

'That's not in the programme,' Emily whispered. Lechasseur nodded.

> *Aer spiritus – I beg thy breath fill its intention,*
> *So thy wind will be hard on the falcon's crest.*
> *Aqua spiritus – I beg its thirst be quenched in thy holy bath,*
> *Court the water, Man and do not be afraid.*

Listening closer, Lechasseur said: 'Sounds like some kind of incantation. And look at him: his skin's gone all pasty.'

Ignus spiritus – I beg thy passion burst, O ardent muse,
As Cionadh's embers rise to greet you.
Terra spiritus – I beg, thy marl cross Adamah,
So instead buried deep, his bones gain strength from thee.

Emily looked around, half-expecting some demon to rise from an unseen corner of the room. But there was nothing odd, other than the confused expressions on the faces of many of the listeners.

Behold, the thought complete!
The logos impressed upon the clay,
Alive the rough beast rises,
Thy head on the body of a lion,
Not in salvation
But in annexation

Bungard, still caught in his half-step, thinking the reading done, was just about to applaud when Randolph Crest screamed loud and long.

'They're here! They're here! They're here!' Crest spat, shaking horribly. 'They've risen and they're coming for me! It's me they want! Not the others!' He reached out stubby fingers to steady himself on the podium, but even that effort proved too much. He slid sideways, then tumbled to the tile floor like a sack of wet laundry. The scrap of paper from which he'd been reading fluttered to the floor beside him.

Bungard was the first by his side, Emily and Lechasseur following quickly along, pressing through the now-standing crowd. Recognising the pair at once from the earlier altercation, Bungard shielded Crest protectively with his own body. 'Stand back, please!' he said, looking directly at Emily and Lechasseur.

'Must be all the excitement,' Lechasseur said. 'Mr Crest leads a very reclusive life. Let us help you get him to the window.'

'No thanks,' Bungard answered. He nodded to two friends in the crowd. They roughly pushed in front of Lechasseur and Emily, forcing them back. Wordlessly, the trio half lifted, half dragged Crest's limp, leaden body over to the somewhat fresher London air that drifted in through the room's tall windows. By the time they had seated him on a bench and loosened his shirt and tie, Crest's breathing had slowed. As the air cooled his sweaty face, his eyelids fluttered, indicating that he was coming to.

Visibly relieved, Bungard rose. 'I'll call an ambulance. Try to clear this place out a bit.' He headed toward the door, muttering: 'Last time I try to pull someone out of semi-retirement. Just not worth it.'

The two men remained with Crest, but Emily and Lechasseur managed to take a few steps closer, bringing them near enough to listen. By the time Bungard had vanished into the hall, Crest's eyes were fully open.

Abruptly, he lurched forward, trying to stand.

'Easy,' one of the men said. 'You've had a fainting spell.'

'I am the rare born,' Crest said, still trying to pull himself up. 'The rare born.' One of the men half-forced him back to a sitting position.

'Look at his eyes,' Emily said. 'He's not awake.'

Indeed, Crest's dilated pupils belonged more to someone dreaming, or hypnotised. The man tried to shift him back a little on the bench, both to make him more comfortable, and to make it harder for him to get up. 'Easy,' the man said, trying to sound comforting. 'Doctors will be here soon.'

But words continued to spew from Crest's lips: 'I see what they can't see, know what they can't know. That's why they want me. That's why they need me. That's why they try to hunt me down, to get me back. I am the rare born. But what are they building? For whom? Leave me! Leave me! Leave me! Take your dirt from my face and my neck! I can't breathe! Get the water out of my mouth! I'm choking! I'm falling! I'm no use to you dead! Leave me! I'm not what I was! I'm not what you want! Who are you bowing to now? Leave!'

Crest's head bobbed lightly back and forth a few times. Then he gasped and collapsed, unconscious again.

The ambulance attendants arrived fifteen minutes later, and, after checking his vitals, packed him off for a trip to hospital.

From outside the old church, Lechasseur watched the flashing ambulance lights retreat into the million small glows of the London night. The audience were dispersing as well, while Bungard explained to stragglers that Mr Crest had been under a lot of stress, and may have had what was known as 'an anxiety attack.'

Emily Blandish, however, standing by Lechasseur's side, was engrossed in reading a scrap of paper.

'What's that?' Lechasseur asked.

'Notes for the last poem he read,' she said, not looking up. 'I nicked it from the floor.'

'As if he's not furious enough with us already!' Lechasseur objected.

'If he's connected to the attacks, it's a clue. If he's not, what difference does it make how angry he is with us?'

'Well,' Lechasseur said, 'we both sense he's connected to *something*!'

Emily sighed, shook her head, then went back to scanning the poem, looking for some sort of clue within it.

Bungard tossed them a curious glance, so Lechasseur grabbed Emily's elbow and began walking her off down the street. Once they were around a corner, she pulled away and headed for a street lamp to give herself some better light.

Honoré threw his hands up in the air. 'Have you even considered the possibility that we're trying to make sense out of nonsense?'

Emily shook her head adamantly. 'Maybe connections don't always play out in straight lines the way most people are used to thinking. Maybe each line of events only makes sense after the fact, and you have to feel your way through . . .'

He turned to the night sky in exasperation. 'Or maybe it's your mind making a pattern when there's really nothing . . . OW!'

He looked back down to see that Emily had reached out in excitement, and had gripped him on the bruised section of his arm.

'Where did Waterman live?' she asked, hurriedly.

'I don't remember the number, off-hand,' Lechasseur said, rubbing his arm. 'The street was . . . Bath Row, I think.'

She shivered visibly. Her gaze didn't waver from the poem.

'And Windleby?' she said, her voice rising nearly an octave.

'Don't remember.'

'Could it be Falcon's Crest?' she asked, slapping his shoulder rapidly with her free hand.

'Maybe. Why?' he said, curiosity rising. 'You're starting to sound a little like Crest, y'know.'

'Look!' she nearly screamed. Then she frantically jabbed her index finger at the handwritten poem. Lechasseur did as he was told, but could barely make out the handwriting. Shaking her head in frustration, she spelled it out for him.

'It's so simple, it's insane! It's right here! *Aer spiritus*, the spirit of the air, the wind will be hard against the falcon's crest! Get it? Windleby! Falcon's Crest! And here, couldn't be any plainer than that!'

'You think Crest's the one behind all this?'

'Well, he's certainly wrapped up in it.'

'Then who's next?'

Her eyes darted down the page again. 'Ardent muse . . . must be Ardent Mews. We've got to find someone named Cionadh living there, or someone named Adamah living on Marl Cross!'

Lechasseur looked up. The sky was black now, the hour approaching that when the Subterraneans usually struck.

'In that case,' he said. 'We'd better be quick about it.'

CHAPTER 8

After all her work, Emily had hoped that Lechasseur could see that she was in no mood to be criticised, but he did not.

'Is this the best London street map you could find?' he complained, the moment she handed it to him. 'It's falling apart, and half the streets on it don't exist!'

'Yes,' she answered. 'It's the best and the only. I'm told a lot of them are like that these days! It's not my fault the street maps haven't caught up with reality.' She grabbed the map back. 'Besides, what have *you* been doing for the last half hour?'

'I did find out that there's an Ardent Mews, but it's in Kensington,' Lechasseur frowned. 'It would take us at least an hour to get there.'

Emily's fingers danced along the little lines on the faded map. 'Look! A Marl Cross in Mayfair! Do we have money for the tube?'

Again, Lechasseur frowned. She stared, perplexed.

'What about the big wad of money that Crest gave you?' she said. Now it was her turn to criticise.

'Back at the flat, I'm afraid.'

'Then how do you propose we get to Marl Cross and stop the murder?'

Lechasseur rolled his hand out regally toward his bicycle.

She stared at him, aghast. He nodded.

Forcing herself up onto the baskets on either side of the rear wheel, Emily held on as best she could to Lechasseur's shoulders as he began a terribly uncomfortable, wobbly ride through London's heedless evening traffic.

After the third time they were nearly broad-sided by a speeding black cab, she shouted: 'I thought *you* were the cautious one!'

'Only about the time-travelling thing,' he called back. 'This part, I'm used to.' He then promptly hit a pothole that almost spilled them into the path of an oncoming bus. After that, she decided it would be best not to speak for the remainder of the trip, and instead to concentrate on maintaining their balance.

Just as Emily's arms began to tire and her grip weaken, Lechasseur skidded to a halt beneath a street sign mounted in the stone façade of a building. Marl Cross. From the looks of it, it was one of those short, pleasant, expensive, exclusive residential roads.

'Now we have to find someone named Adamah along the next mile and a half of houses,' she said, rubbing the spots on her backside made most sore by the wild ride.

'It'd be faster and easier to look for the Subterraneans,' Lechasseur said, chaining his bike to some nearby railings.

'Adamah . . . ' Emily stretched and rolled the name on her tongue. 'It's Hebrew, isn't it? And it probably means earth.'

The street was quiet. Lechasseur, looking terribly out of place in his trench coat, but seemingly unaware of it, walked slowly down the centre of the road, scanning for sweet wrappers. Emily moved steadily behind him, her pace slowed by a newfound pain in her lower back. They passed a locked park, and several white buildings, all the while looking for shredded wrappers.

Halfway down the street, having found not so much as a single wrapper, bitten or otherwise, Lechasseur stopped. 'Nothing here,' he said. 'Maybe we should double back and check the manhole covers. Or maybe we should ask some of the neighbours for a Mr, Mrs, or Miss Adamah.' He rubbed the back of his head.

Emily looked up at the windows of the houses. A few had lights behind the curtains, but just as many were dark. She wasn't at all sure what they would say if they did knock at any of the doors. 'I've just realised,' she said. 'The addresses are tied in, too. Marl means some sort of dirt, doesn't it?

Lechasseur shrugged.

'Earth . . . dirt,' Emily wondered aloud. 'How would you kill someone with dirt?'

'Dump it on them,' Lechasseur offered. 'Bury them.' Suddenly he snapped his fingers and whirled round. 'We passed a park, didn't we?'

By the time Emily nodded, he was running back down the street towards the gated park. She could already see, from where she was, that there was something wrong with the curled iron gate. It seemed half off its hinges.

Lechasseur, meanwhile, picked up speed, as if to jump the fence when he reached it. Emily, struggling to catch up, turned her attention to the interior, to the shadows of the low, pruned trees and the deeper darknesses within the park. She noticed, in particular, a group of thick shadows. At first, she took them for a row of bushes, until she noticed with a gasp that, as Lechasseur was moving towards the gate, they were moving out to meet him.

'Look out!' she called. But instead of drawing his attention to the danger, the cry made him turn back toward her.

'No! No! The park!' she shouted.

Panicked, she gritted her teeth against the pain in her back and picked up her speed, just as the shadows reached him. He'd barely turned to face them as they passed. It was the Subterraneans all right – hairy, oily, bestial, and moving at a blinding speed. Emily held her breath, but, oddly, rather than attack, or even try to pinion them as they had so easily in Windleby's flat, this time the creatures simply barrelled past, their goal a manhole in the street a few yards away.

They jumped and pulled over one another; a matted, hairy mass of skinny but powerful arms and legs that scrabbled and tore in a frantic effort to reach the manhole first.

'Look how erratic they are!' Emily called, slowing her pace. 'This isn't like last time.'

Lechasseur noticed it, too, and stood stock-still as they raced passed him.

'Might mean we're too late,' he said.

All at once, she saw his face tighten.

'But, I've got an idea,' he said. 'Stay there.'

Slowly, Lechasseur made his way over to the gate. There, with both hands, he firmly grabbed and twisted free an iron rod that had been bent out of shape by the rush of the creatures. Then he waited.

Ten . . . fifteen . . . twenty of the creatures skidded, slid and clawed their way from the park to the sewer as Lechasseur and Emily stood and watched. At first they came five or six at a time. Then the size of the groups shrank to three or four, then two or three. Just as what appeared to be the last three creatures leapt for the sewer, Lechasseur stepped forward and swung the rod, catching one of them on the side of its head.

The creature flew sideways, staggered briefly, then righted itself and started racing for the sewer again, apparently none the worse for the blow. But then, as its two fellows squeezed past it, it suddenly rose straight up, then tumbled backward, heaving from side to side. Confused, it turned left, then right. It made a whining sound, like a baby, then collapsed.

Lechasseur called to Emily. 'See any rope anywhere? Anything we can use as rope?'

She shook her head, then, realising he wasn't looking at her, called out: 'No.'

Shrugging, he took off his leather coat and pulled off his shirt, briefly revealing his strong, but not over-muscled, coffee-brown shoulders and chest. There were some scars, but whether they were knife or bullet wounds, or from something else entirely, Emily couldn't tell. She watched him curiously, never having seen her normally-guarded partner so physically vulnerable.

As if feeling a chill, he put the coat back on. Then, with a pained sigh, he tore the shirt into a series of long strips, which he used to bind the creature's hands and feet. It was still alive, breathing with what he guessed was a normal rhythm. Emily stepped up and saw a large swelling on the back of its head where the iron rod had struck.

Emily watched as Lechasseur rolled the creature into a puddle of light from the nearest street-lamp. A sweet, sweaty smell rolled across her, making her gag and forcing her to step back.

Pulling back himself, Lechasseur remarked: 'Take a close look. He's as ugly as Crest.'

But Emily wasn't listening. She'd spotted a five foot tall mound of fresh dirt in the park, built up into a pile in the middle of a paved stone walk. She moved closer and realised that the whitish object atop the pile was not a piece of clothing, or a flag, but a naked, bloody foot and ankle.

CHAPTER 9

The creature was awake now, its wide eyes pivoting madly as if unable to make sense of the small flat that was its prison. The wiry thing bucked and twisted in the chair. Although its feet were tied above the ground, it arched its back with such force that the whole chair lifted and fell half a foot at a time. Lechasseur and Emily watched, worried that the chair might splinter at any moment.

Lechasseur reached forward, planning to hold the chair down physically, at least until the thing tired itself out. But the creature snapped its neck around and, with the speed of a sprung mousetrap, champed down hard, only narrowly missing the tips of Lechasseur's fingers.

Lechasseur pulled back immediately. 'Okay,' he muttered. 'Not going to try that again.'

The thing snapped its mouth threateningly a few more times and emitted a low guttural growl.

A ruddy sun was beginning to show over the building tops. It'd been a long night's work dragging the creature and Lechasseur's bicycle back here, and it was no surprise that morning was now arriving. Lechasseur stepped over to the windows and pulled the curtains closed.

Emily rolled her eyes. 'Must you?' she asked from the far side of the room. Quite determined to keep her distance from the thing, she was leaning against the wall, pretending not to be trying to press herself through it. The rising sun had offered welcome relief from the preceding hours of desperation and gloom.

'Not for me, this time,' he said. 'I'm not the only lover of darkness here, and we don't want to upset our friend any more than we have to.'

Though the creature still rattled about, the respite from even the dull light of dawn mollified it considerably. Its eyes moved from Lechasseur to Emily, then back again, as if finally seeing them for the first time.

'Can you see anything about it?' Emily asked – meaning, he knew, its path in time.

'Not yet,' he said, edging a bit closer.

'Maybe you should . . . try,' she said. 'Practice a bit.'

Lechasseur stopped short. 'I've no idea how,' he protested. 'It just happens. You know that.'

'But maybe it only happens that way because you're afraid of it. Maybe it happens quite naturally, all the time, but when it usually does, you hold it back.'

'Could be,' Lechasseur said. 'Unfortunately, I get tense just thinking about it.'

'Let go,' she encouraged. 'Stare at it. Relax your eyes and let them go blurry. After all, it's not as though we can ask it much of anything.'

Wordlessly agreeing, Lechasseur raised and lowered his shoulders to relax them a bit, then exhaled and stared at the creature.

It was human, but not quite. The eyes were too big, the loose, leathery skin too dark with both hair and a black, greasy oil. He could see why the newspapers had dubbed them cavemen, or troglodytes, but even those labels didn't capture the sense of the creature before them. Living underground had given it and its kin a more reptilian slant than those words implied.

After scanning the creature's face, Lechasseur took a deep breath and looked it in the eyes. Surprisingly, this seemed to calm it more, and it returned the gaze with equal curiosity. Lechasseur found himself staring across a gulf into the heart of another species.

Lechasseur had stared at caged tigers eye to eye, at pet birds, dogs and cats. He'd also stared at good friends, and at men he was just about to kill. But this experience wasn't like any of those. The look the creature gave him wasn't the blank and pitiless gaze of a caged tiger, nor the intelligent, more piercing look of a fellow human. Oh, there was definitely something else there, seeing him, feeling him, measuring him. It was deep, but not entirely sympathetic. Lechasseur just didn't know what to call it.

Remembering his goal, he tried to relax some more, to let his view of the creature go slightly blurry, and see what else came up. After a moment, a strange vertigo hit him. The scene before him split in two, and the half-world where worms of time took up space began to envelop his senses.

He saw the three of them rolling backwards, out of the flat, back to the murder scene. He saw the creature hiding in the dark with its brothers as he and Emily passed by the first time. But then, all at once, a shrill whine filled its head, and Lechasseur's ears: a rush like gallons of water, only made up not of drops but of voices, not speaking English, or any other recognisable language, but issuing commands and demands in images and screeches of hunger and need.

If the distortion of time was disorientating, this indecipherable cacophony was all too much. Unable even to tell where it began and ended, Lechasseur pulled back with a hoarse scream. The creature, for its part, either sensing what Lechasseur had sensed, or simply reacting to his sudden sound and movement, began frantically jumping and pulling anew at its bonds.

Lechasseur felt Emily's hands around his shoulders, heard her voice asking: 'What happened? Honoré? Are you all right?'

Lechasseur grasped his head in his hands. 'It was like . . . like . . . It was being one thing, thinking one way one minute, and then all of a sudden, it was something completely different. Something louder, stronger.'

'Honoré,' Emily said, a note of fear in her voice.

He turned and saw that the creature's stamping had cracked one of the chair's legs, and was threatening to shatter it.

'No, no, none of that!' Lechasseur said, as if talking to a naughty pet. He crossed shakily to the kitchen area and began to rummage about in a cupboard.

Emily watched the creature with growing trepidation as it smashed about harder and harder. She wondered if perhaps Lechasseur's mind had been lost off down some time trail, but he re-emerged a few seconds later, holding aloft a wrapped bar of chocolate.

'This time,' he said, pulling the treat free from the foil, 'you can enjoy it without the wrapper.'

The thing saw, or smelled, the chocolate immediately, and jostled about with increased fury. Emily was certain that its bonds would give way any second, but Lechasseur screamed and pointed at it.

'AHHH!' he shouted.

It stopped and stared.

Lechasseur put his fingers to his lips and said: 'Shhh!' Then he pointed to the chocolate.

Its brow furrowed. It began stamping again.

'AHHH!' Lechasseur shouted again. Again it stopped, and again he put his fingers to his lips and said: 'Shhh!'

This time it remained stationary, panting, its gaze moving forlornly between Lechasseur and the chocolate.

Lechasseur smiled and said: 'Good.'

Then he held the bar towards its mouth. It jumped forward and snapped off a large chunk of chocolate. Lechasseur, still fearful for his fingers, pulled his hand back quickly. It was ignoring him now, though; chewing and making little grunting noises that both Emily and Lechasseur understood to indicate pleasure.

'Maybe I should spread some papers under the chair,' Lechasseur said grimly. 'I doubt he's house trained.'

Still chewing, the thing looked up and gave Lechasseur a toothy grin, full of rotted teeth, with shards of saliva-wet chocolate visible in between.

'I think it likes you,' Emily chuckled.

'Next time, I'll let *you* feed it, then. Just so it doesn't develop any favourites.' Lechasseur tossed the remaining piece of chocolate into the creature's open mouth. 'We'd also better buy some more sweets.'

'You were communicating pretty effectively,' Emily said. 'Something you saw?'

'Maybe,' Lechasseur shrugged. 'Just an instinct, but these days I'm never really sure where they come from. I was fine following it back all the way to the park, but then something . . . possessed it, or rose up from inside it.'

'Whatever's been controlling them?' Emily guessed.

'It seemed more natural than that, like it was a part of it. Just not a part that worked in any way that I understood. Almost like it was sort of . . . outside time . . .' Lechasseur's voice trailed off as he realised he was no longer certain what he was getting at.

'Maybe you should try again,' Emily said. 'There is still one murder to go.'

'Or maybe one of us should be heading over to Ardent Mews to find this poor Cionadh person before it's too late,' he replied. 'I would like to be able to stop at least one killing.'

'But then what do we do with your house guest?' Emily asked.

'He seems pretty happy now. Maybe I can snag a box of chocolate. It's what I do, after all. Then we can spread out a lot of papers, chain him to the pipes and leave him here. He'll probably be happy as a clam.'

They both turned to the creature just in time watch its grin vanish, its limbs sag and its pupils dilate. Once again it started jumping in the chair, not frantically this time, but rhythmically, with a steady, machine-like pulse.

'What's that about?' Lechasseur wondered aloud.

Emily, forgetting her instinctual fear, stepped forward. 'You're right. It's not an outside force, it is natural.'

'What's natural?'

Emily knelt down by the chair, and Lechasseur put his hand on her shoulder, ready to pull her back, but she brushed it away. 'Leave me alone a moment. I can hear it.'

'Hear what?' Lechasseur knew that at times Emily was capable of an amazing intuition that bordered on telepathy. Now it seemed she was crossing the border. After some tense moments, she pulled back.

'It's like a beehive,' she said. 'A hive mind.'

Lechasseur furrowed his brow. 'A what?'

'Scientists say that a beehive is like an individual organism, with each bee in it acting not as an individual, but as a part of a sort of single being, a single mind. The Subterraneans are more sophisticated than that. They have their own mind, but at times this sort of communal over-mind takes over, directing all their actions at once. Have you heard of Carl Jung, the psychiatrist? He said: "Don't you know if you get one hundred of the most intelligent people in the world together, they're a stupid mob? Ten thousand would have the collective intelligence of an alligator." This would be the opposite.'

'Doesn't say much for mankind, but that explains how the Subterraneans could be so organised during the attack, and so disorganised once it was over,' Lechasseur mused. 'Is this communal mind arranging the ritual, then?'

'Not sure,' Emily answered. 'We could try touching the creature and jumping along his time trail.'

Lechasseur shook his head. 'Who knows where we'd wind up or for how long? Maybe trapped underground with a hundred of his hungry friends. And it's certainly not going to save the fourth victim.'

At first she thought he was simply being resistant, as usual, to making a jump, but she had to admit his reasons were sound. 'Then maybe you should have another look.'

'I told you, it gets too noisy,' he protested.

'Maybe now that you know what it is, it'll be different,' she said. 'Look, the chair's holding, it's thumping along like a cog in a wheel. Maybe you can see what this uni-mind, or whatever you want to call it, is up to.'

'All right,' Lechasseur answered. 'All right.'

He put his finger to his lips to try to hush the creature again, but it was no use. Even the strange intelligence he'd previously sensed in its eyes was gone, leaving behind this uncomprehending automaton.

Lechasseur sighed and let his eyes go blurry again. The steady drumming of the chair against the floor helped it all come easier, perhaps because it made one moment seem exactly like the one before it and the one after it. The time worm rapidly emerged from the creature, but on this occasion headed not into the past, but into the future. The worm writhed and twisted, growing out in all directions, the more familiar three-dimensional reality played along its sides almost like a picture show.

Lechasseur saw the creature there, surrounded by sweets and paper, then it was led in near pitch blackness along a dank sewer by a chain. An odd gradation rolled along the outside of the worm, and Lechasseur realised that the light and location were changing.

They were in a tiny workman's flat. The furnishings were meagre. An end table with the day's papers and the evening's post. The creatures were here, too, twenty to thirty strong. He could smell as well as see them. He even caught a glimpse of what he thought must be himself lying on the floor near the front door, pinned by the creatures, a chain still held tightly in his hand. Nearby, a powerful man was being lifted, then carried.

This is it, then, Lechasseur thought. *The next murder!*

With a desperate ripple of old frustration, he reasoned that there was nothing he could do for himself or the victim in this shadow land of perception.

Or was there?

With the utmost effort, Lechasseur managed to swerve his point of view deeper into the worm, away from the carnage and toward the pile of letters on the table. With a satisfied sigh, he managed to hurl his consciousness back into the present, where Emily was waiting.

'Did you see?' she asked. 'Did you find out the purpose of the ritual?'

'No,' he said. 'But, I did see two things. First, this time, it didn't look like they killed the victim. I think they kidnapped him. And I managed to spot the address. The Ardent Mews we're looking for isn't the one on the map in Kensington at all. It's in Holborn.'

CHAPTER 10

Thanks to the prodigious down-payment from Crest, which they realised might well be his life savings, Lechasseur had managed to procure at short notice from his suppliers some heavy chains, a large box of chocolates and a second electric torch with new batteries. Emily had meanwhile strewn newspapers about the flat in sufficient quantity to cover a third of the floor. With their primal guest tightly secured, and apparently quite content with the box of sweets, the duo quickly made their way by tube train to Holborn station, and from there to Ardent Mews.

The smart street was clean and well-cared for; that is to say, with the notable exception of number 93, home of Mr Brae Cionadh, Irishman by birth, warehouse foreman by trade. One of the house's two front windows had been boarded up with wood. The other had two cracked panes. Cionadh was in much the same dilapidated state as his home. He responded to the knocking at his door quickly enough, his ruddy face scowling out at Lechasseur and Emily from beneath a thick shock of fiery red hair. He wore a torn, stained vest that barely contained a thick combination of chest muscles and belly fat. Lechasseur and Emily were well aware that any attempt to persuade the uninitiated that their life was in imminent danger from a horde of Troglodytes would be difficult, but they also quickly realised that convincing Mr Cionadh would be a particular challenge.

Trying to imagine what words from a stranger he might himself heed, Lechasseur spoke slowly and carefully about 'a matter of grave importance.'

Throughout his little speech, Cionadh angled his green eyes down at some point in the middle of Lechasseur's chest. He breathed heavily but steadily, in a manner not unlike the Subterranean they'd left behind. Sensing a pause in Lechasseur's words, Cionadh looked up. Lechasseur noticed a yellowish tinge at the edges of the man's eyes and wondered if perhaps he was ill.

'Drink?' Cionadh said, though it scarcely sounded like a word. With that, all three went inside.

The flat looked exactly as Lechasseur had seen in his vision, only the human smell was thicker now, and he found himself wishing that the windows were open, not necessarily for the light, but for the air.

Cionadh handed Lechasseur a crusty glass, quarter filled with amber liquid. Lechasseur accepted, but only sipped at the contents, which he swore more closely resembled kerosene than any drinkable spirit. Emily refused hers, which immediately marked her, in Cionadh's eyes, as deeply suspicious. Cionadh downed her glass, then his own, then slumped into a wooden chair that seemed far too small for his size.

Emily remained silent, while Lechasseur tried to talk about the danger without actually talking about it. Cionadh seemed to be listening, but then occasionally waved his hand in front of his face as if Lechasseur was some insect that he was trying to swat away.

Not sure that he was making his point, Lechasseur became more and more explicit, and more and more frustrated that he didn't seem to be getting through. Finally, puffing himself up a bit more than he intended, Lechasseur said: 'Mr Cionadh, what I'm trying to say is that you're in a great deal of trouble.'

Responding to what he imagined as Lechasseur's aggressive stance, Cionadh rolled forward. 'I think,' he drawled, 'the only one in trouble here . . . is you!'

Cionadh stood up and pushed Lechasseur hard in the shoulder with two stiff fingers. Trying to keep things from getting completely out of control, Lechasseur smiled as pleasantly as he could and shook his head.

'No, please. You don't understand. I don't want to fight you. We're just here to help you!'

'Don't want to fight? You're afraid of me then, you bastard coward?' Cionadh spat. Flecks of saliva spattered Lechasseur's face.

Lechasseur stepped back and raised his hands, palms out, in a supplicating gesture.

'Please, Mr Cionadh,' he said.

'This isn't going at all well,' commented Emily.

Lechasseur glanced at her, and Cionadh took the opportunity to punch him in the side of the face with the full force of his thick right arm. Lechasseur's head snapped to the side, followed by his shoulders, his waist and his legs. Then he crashed to the ground.

He awoke a few minutes later with Emily pressing a cold cloth to the side of his jaw. It was numb now, but swelling. He knew it would be hurting a lot very soon. Gingerly, he probed the inside of his mouth with his tongue, to see if any teeth were loose. Satisfied that they were all accounted for, he looked at Emily and said: 'Where's . . . ?' But he found he could no longer manage to pronounce 'Cionadh' without wincing from the pain in his jaw.

Emily knew what he meant, however, and nodded towards the middle of the room. Frustrated beyond belief, Lechasseur shook his head as he stared at Cionadh, bound and gagged in the wooden chair.

'Now what do we do? Bring him back to the flat as well? Start a collection?' Lechasseur complained. The thrumming in his jaw made him stop and press the compress to his face even harder.

Emily was apologetic. 'I'm sorry! He was going to hurt you! I had to do something!'

'What *did* you do?'

Emily looked coyly at Lechasseur. 'I may look harmless . . .' She smiled and waved at a pile of broken crockery in the corner. 'Never did like ornamental teapots anyway.'

Lechasseur rose, turned his back on their newest prisoner and waved off Emily's concern. 'Oh, you didn't do anything wrong, Emily. He's a lout, probably pissed since the War ended. It's just . . . we've got to get him out of here, soon, and we can't very well go dragging him through the streets in broad daylight!'

Cionadh had other ideas, however. As soon as he saw that Lechasseur's back was to him, he lifted himself up on his feet and charged him, like a bull. He and Lechasseur slammed into the front door, which cracked, splintered, and barely slowed their tumble.

Several hours later, Emily and Lechasseur left Holborn police station,

Lechasseur somewhat the worse for wear.

'At least they didn't keep us in the cells overnight,' Emily pointed out.

Lechasseur, clutching his jaw with one hand and his side with the other, didn't want to respond.

'And you can't really blame the neighbours for calling the police,' she went on. 'They had no idea who we were.' She lowered her voice as she saw two bobbies approaching from the opposite direction. 'I did my best to explain, but apparently we're not the only ones making extraordinary claims about the Subterraneans. The desk sergeant said it had become something of a fad.'

Lechasseur winced and mumbled. 'Just . . . wish they'd arrested . . . Cionadh, too. For protection.'

'Right. It's getting late. We'd better get back there, fast, then.'

But as they stepped briskly past the two bobbies, they overheard one say to the other: 'That's right. They didn't kill him. I don't know why, but they didn't kill him.'

Hearing that, Lechasseur whispered: 'Too late.'

They walked quickly along, Lechasseur limping just a bit, gaining distance so that the two officers would not overhear.

'Maybe they're taking him somewhere to complete the ritual?' Emily said.

'Sure, in the vision. But the future's all changed now, isn't it? When I saw it, our captive had led us there, like a dog on a leash. That's how we knew where to go, but we were too late. This time, we weren't even near the big event. Knowing what was going to happen changed what happened. So, who knows what really happened?'

Emily shook her head, trying to wrap it around Lechasseur's grammar. 'All right, yes. Things are changed, but if it's a proper ritual it still has to be performed the same way, doesn't it? And probably at the same place?'

'Maybe. But how do we figure out where they've taken him?'

'Well, there's our friend back at the flat,' she pointed out. 'You said yourself that it led us to Cionadh's house. Why not the ritual site?'

Lechasseur nodded, winced, then looked at her. 'Are we allowed to get ideas like that, from the future? Isn't that a contradiction?'

'Don't know. Let's see.' Emily strode toward the nearest entrance to the tube, and Lechasseur followed.

CHAPTER 11

Emily knew that some time during London's long, rich, deep, intricate history, there must have been stranger sights. But, as she and Lechasseur sloshed through the sewer, pulled along through brown-green muck by a long chain attached to the ankle of their captive Subterranean, she was at a loss to imagine anything more peculiar.

'Hold the torch down,' Lechasseur said.

'What good is it, pointed down?' Emily objected. 'As it is, we can barely see.'

Ever since she'd agreed that, since Lechasseur was the stronger, he should keep both hands on the chain, while she managed the light, he'd been advising her about where to point it. Now, Emily was getting somewhat annoyed.

'The light is confusing it,' he answered. 'Making it harder for it to see.'

Sure enough, the creature's eyes, though hypnotically dilated, wobbled back and forth. Its brow was also scrunched.

'It probably smells the extra chocolate bar you brought in your pocket,' she suggested.

Lechasseur shook his head. 'Don't think so. At least try pointing it down, please?'

Sighing, she dutifully did as requested, loathe to relinquish the only thing that enabled her to get her bearings in this dismal place. The pale light made a long oval that shone yellow against the browns and greens on the concrete ledge that they were following. Instantly, the creature's pace picked up, as if the light had been dampening its sense of smell and now it could catch the scent. Emily was impressed. Lechasseur's intuition was paying off more and more, as if his fears and depression were waning and he was beginning to trust himself. Or, she thought again, his inner troubles were at least weakened by distraction.

When they'd returned to the flat, a few bleary-eyed neighbours had eyed Lechasseur angrily, making them worry that their house guest had escaped. But it, and most of the furniture, had still been present and accounted for. Quite a lot had been broken, though, including the sleep of Lechasseur's neighbours. Sneaking the creature out had been considerably more difficult than subduing it. A rug folded into a sack, tied together at the top, had sufficed until they could find a quiet alley in which to release it. Though the rug had been ugly and torn to begin with, Lechasseur had briefly bemoaned the loss of the only thing that had covered the huge stains and loose wooden floorboards in his living space.

Once free, obeying the unheard siren-song of the group mind, the thing had trotted along on all fours, then led them down the nearest sewer opening. It was a peculiar blessing that the uni-mind state seemed to slow it down a bit. They were already moving as quickly as they could, and would have been unable to keep up if the creature had been progressing at even half its top speed. With the torch light muted, it moved along happily, only occasionally tugging at the chain. Emily imagined with a smile that they must look every bit the handsome young couple taking their cheery, over-sized, over-eager Airedale out for a pleasant underground muck-stroll.

The smile faded with the passing time. She soon found herself starting to struggle for breath.

Perhaps noticing, Lechasseur, panting a bit himself, broke the silence. 'The sewers cover at least as big an area as London itself. But you know, getting there will be only the start of our problems. We're most likely heading straight into a horde of them, remember?'

'Even that,' Emily said, steeling herself for a still longer ordeal, 'would be preferable to this stench!'

'Ah. I think I can see some kind of intersection ahead. Maybe we're getting somewhere.' Lechasseur rewrapped a loose bit of chain tightly around his upper arm for a better grip.

Emily tried to widen her eyes to let in more light, hoping to see what he saw. The view was blurry, but up the tunnel, illuminated by the dull circles of light provided by the regularly-placed manhole covers in the arched ceiling, the path seemed to split. As they approached, she could see that the right side led upwards, while the left descended further into the dark.

As Emily wondered why she should be at all surprised, the creature sloshed off down the darker path. A hundred yards further on, it deftly found a group of iron rungs set into the stone wall, and clambered down, spider-like, to even greater depths. Lechasseur had to struggle to avoid getting the chain tangled on the rungs. As Emily watched, she realised that the darkness below was absolute, and she could see nothing at all.. Her face, however, was being fanned by a blast of warmer, slightly cleaner air rising up from the hole. It made her sweat, but let her breathe a little deeper. In the distance, she could hear the sound of rushing water, mixed with something else.

Lechasseur heard it, too. 'Must be near one of the main outlets,' he said.

But Emily was trying to ignore the rushing water, concentrating on the something else. 'Shh!' she said, as she realised what it was. She grabbed his shoulder and added in whisper: 'Listen! Can't you hear it?'

'Just the water . . .'

'No, chanting,' Emily said.

The chain rattled as the creature's tugging became more insistent, and they set off after it. Moving apparently only on the basis of sound now in the inky darkness, it turned left down one invisible tunnel, then right down another. The water sloshed up to Emily's ankles even on the ledge, making her grateful that she couldn't see it.

At first, she mistook what they saw next for the flashes of colour one sees when one's eyes are shut tight. Far off in the field of utter black that their vision had become, a muted golden glow appeared in the shape of a rectangle. As they approached, she recognised it as a grate in the wall, beyond which was a lit area. To the right of the grate was a circular opening: apparently the way in.

'That settles it,' Emily whispered as they approached. 'There is someone or something other than our hairy friends involved. *They* wouldn't need any light.'

'Umf!' Lechasseur answered, as the creature lurched forward.

Emily heard a splash and some curses and realised that the creature had pulled her friend down onto his knees, soaking even more of his trousers. Fearing he needed help, she shone the flashlight toward him. She watched as the creature, sensing its nearness to its goal, pulled all the harder, stretching the long, bony fingers of its hands towards the opening near the grate.

Lechasseur, still unbalanced, span sideways on the ledge and nearly tumbled into the deeper water that filled the channel. 'Give me a hand . . . ' he spat.

Emily grabbed the chain and pulled it toward the wall, hoping to find something to hook it onto and give her some leverage. But the creature's will, buffeted by the communal urges of its fellows, was adamantine. Before she could reach the wall or Lechasseur, its hands found the edges of the entrance, and pulled for all they were worth.

The chain slipped from Emily's hand. She realised at once that this left Lechasseur with two choices; he could either be yanked into the midst of a large group of Troglodytes and whatever else was inside, or let go of his end of the chain.

He chose to let go.

In a flash, the creature vanished into the entrance tunnel. They both watched as the last few feet of chain rattled against the lower lip of the stone circle, then clattered off into the chamber beyond.

Lechasseur sat up and looked at Emily. 'This can't be good for my leather coat,' he said. For a moment, she thought he was trying to sound cheerful.

'It's better this way,' Emily whispered, hoping her voice sounded comforting. 'We couldn't very well go charging into the crowd, could we?'

She raised the torch to get a better look at her partner, then reached out her free hand and helped him to his feet. His clothes dripped, and he ineffectually tried to wring water from his coat. Then he turned back to the grate and said: 'Let's have a look, then, shall we?'

Emily nodded, lowered the torch, and moved up right behind him, peering into the space beyond.

CHAPTER 12

The first thing Emily saw were Subterraneans, lots of them, perhaps as many as a hundred, all sitting, crowded together on the tiered concrete ledges of a large, open drainage room. The chanting was coming from them, she realised. Their low, subdued voices sounded more human at a distance, though even now, the indecipherable moans were regular enough at least to seem as if they were composed of words. A continual splashing was still muffling the chant. Emily noticed that several tall pipes opened in the walls, dribbling their contents onto a wide floor where the water was a few feet deep.

In the throes of their communal psyche, the creatures nodded rhythmically, in unison, making them look to Emily like a grotesque parody of the mechanical displays she had once seen in the windows of Harrods.

The second thing she noticed was Cionadh, bound, gagged and tied to the base of a statue mounted in the central pool. Bundles of sticks and cardboard boxes had been piled around him for an obvious purpose. His name, after all, meant child of fire, while Ardent, that of the street where he lived, meant burning. He seemed oddly calm, and Emily wondered if he was lucky enough to think himself dreaming.

The statue, though the last part of the bizarre scene on which she focused, was the most striking of all. It looked to be made of some sort of ebon stone carved into the shape of a horned demon, its visage made no less terrifying by the fact that Emily was certain she'd seen it before, if only in a corner of her worst nightmare.

The light in the chamber was dimmer than the glowing grate had led her to believe. It was provided by a few open flames that crackled and twirled in gold, silver and bronze in two stone braziers on either side of the statue.

Standing behind the statue was a long, lean figure that Emily noticed only because it had started to move. It was either totally in shadow, or dressed in back. It was taller, thinner than the creatures, obviously human. The hint of curves, and the glint of long, straight, combed and pampered black hair, instantly revealed it to be the figure of a woman. She moved smoothly, had an almost feline quality. She shifted about behind the braziers, working on something, revealing more curves as her hips undulated briefly into the flickering light.

At that moment, Lechasseur's foot slipped on the ledge, and he grabbed at the grating for support to stop himself falling into the water. It shifted with a scraping sound that echoed loudly around the enclosed space.

'Who is there? Who dares?'

The loud commanding voice, possessed of a condescending English-rose accent and tinged at the edges with the unmistakable timbre of power, carried easily over the chanting. The woman stepped into the light of the braziers, revealing skin so white that it was almost blue, and bright red lips. Her close-fitting black gown was edged with a deep red fringe.

Emily stared at her in astonishment. The woman's eyes were blue, the whites flecked with gold spots that glittered hypnotically in the dim light.

The bulb in Emily's electric torch sizzled and popped, breaking the spell.

'Mestizer,' Lechasseur mumbled.

Emily knew the name. A hypnotist, a mystic, a powerful creature with many followers, all somehow mixed up in the mystery of how Emily had come to be in London in the first place.

'Come here,' Mestizer commanded. 'Come here now, or I'll have my friends shred you like paper.'

Emily tensed. Should they run for it? She hoped that Lechasseur would be able to come up with some clever strategy that her own frightened mind could not.

'Go in,' Lechasseur whispered.

'*What?*' Emily nearly screeched.

'She probably won't know who you are. She'll want to talk about why you're here. Distract her. I'll be right behind you. As soon as I'm close enough, I'll open the flood-gates. At least it'll put out the fire.'

'What do you mean . . . ?' Emily began. Then she saw where he was pointing.

Set in the wall, not far from where they stood, was a tall, round drain opening covered by a metal hatch. The control wheel for the hatch was mounted next to it on the wall. From the way the water dripped from the top and bottom of the hatch, it was clear that there was a considerable amount of pressure behind it.

Emily understood at once and nodded.

'All right,' she called through the grate. 'I'm coming in.'

'Wise choice,' Mestizer said.

Emily entered the tunnel, feeling the presence of Lechasseur close behind. 'Once you're in,' he whispered, 'get as far away from that drain as you can. Try to get her to keep her eyes on you.'

Moving slowly, so as not to trip, Emily made her way into the dim light of the braziers. As she entered, she could finally make out, to her surprise, that the creatures were chanting words, English words, familiar words:

Ignus spiritus – I beg thy passion burst, O ardent muse,
As Cionadh's embers rise to greet you

'Crest's poem,' Emily realised. 'Then he *is* connected to all this.'

Enticing though the information was, there were more immediate concerns. Mestizer stepped forward to get a better view of Emily, then demanded, once again: 'Who are you?'

Remembering Lechasseur's instructions, Emily climbed down a few tiers of concrete, then started moving to the left, pretending she was retreating from Mestizer out of timid fear.

Mestizer opened her eyes wide, as if sucking in every detail that made Emily what she was. Then, all at once, apparently shocked by something she saw, Mestizer pulled back and whispered: 'You can't be! It's so absurd! Here? Now?'

Emily stared at the woman, who seemed dizzy with whatever knowledge she'd gleaned. Mestizer lowered her forehead to her arm and emitted a series of surprised noises that made her sound somewhat like the Subterraneans. Then, almost immediately, she raised her head again and said: 'And you know Lechasseur! Is he here as well? He must be!'

This was bad news. If Mestizer could read minds, it might be only seconds before she accidentally gave away Lechasseur's presence and intentions. But Mestizer, without bothering to wait for an answer, began to cackle, then laugh almost hysterically. It seemed to Emily that the tall woman's mind couldn't quite focus, and was leaping from one thought to another.

The emotional spasm at an end for the moment, Mestizer turned toward Emily, who was now several yards from the sealed drainage tunnel. Mestizer's nostrils briefly flared, then she managed a slight, pained smile. 'Do you know, little thing, that had you and I met before, had you simply come to me, all this . . . all this . . . *extreme* effort, would have been utterly unnecessary?'

'What do you mean?' Emily asked.

'Must I spell it out for you? In some ways, some *special* ways, I'm just like your handsome friend,' she said. 'And I need, very badly, someone like you. Understand?'

She's a time sensitive, Emily realised. *Just like Honoré and that man Radford. And she wants a channeller.*

Mestizer stepped closer, giving Emily an excuse to move even further from the sealed drain. As Mestizer moved, she spoke, eyes wild and wide. 'Once in a great while, believe it or not, a leader is born among our underground friends here. Someone who helps them to find their way in their little world. Unfortunately, they managed to lose their last one, probably ate him. Ever since, they've been looking for a replacement. When I realised that their group Mind perceives time in a non-linear fashion – something Lechasseur must have sensed as well, by now – I saw a mutual solution to our needs. So, I offered to give their communal psyche a physical form through the use of an ancient spell. As you've doubtless realised, the partnership has been most successful, though I daresay that the Mind itself is much more interested in the outcome than its subjects are. Where is Lechasseur, by the way? Hiding in the tunnels somewhere? How ungallant to send a girl to do his dirty work!'

There was only a few feet between them now. Emily could sense a wave of energy crackling from Mestizer, similar to the sensation she sometimes got from Lechasseur, but much stronger and much darker.

'A manifestation of the Mind?' Emily said, prodding her on.

'Oh, must I spell it out? Since it doesn't perceive time in the limited way that most humans do, if given form, it would be the perfect . . .'

'Time channeller.'

'Bright girl,' Mestizer said, sarcastically. 'These poor creatures get the king they've longed for, I get my atemporal dance partner, all with a little help from the four primal elemental powers of the world.'

'You killed three men for that?' Emily asked.

Mestizer widened her eyes and nodded vigorously. 'Of course, my dear. Morality is different from a wider perspective. One could argue that, given their names and addresses, they were destined to fulfil a greater purpose.'

'And by "greater purpose", you mean yours,' Emily said, trying to keep her talking, wondering why Lechasseur hadn't already made his move.

Again Mestizer nodded vigorously. 'My purpose, and, I suppose,' she added with a sneer, 'the purpose of being old king log for these frogs.'

The Subterraneans continued their chanting. Mestizer had stopped talking, and the water had yet to come crashing down. Emily had to say something, something distracting. Mestizer was already looking away, scanning the walls.

'You realise we're going to try to stop you,' Emily announced haughtily.

Mestizer slowly turned back to Emily and looked levelly at her. Emily saw the light from the fires reflected in her eyes. And as she looked, she saw the gold flecks twinkle. Pretty gold flecks.

'That's right, little thing,' whispered Mestizer, in a voice like honey. 'Look into my eyes.'

Emily looked, and found she could not look away. Mestizer's gaze pinned her, and the woman's eyes were the most beautiful thing she could ever remember seeing.

At that moment, there was a scuffle of movement behind her as Lechasseur leapt up from where he had been hiding, caught the wheel and, with a few quick turns, started to open the drain. A wall of murky water cascaded from the opening, growing with every moment as the hatch swung open. It crashed down into the room, drenching Cionadh, pushing most of the cardboard and kindling away into the drains, and pouring around the demon statue.

The Subterraneans, though some were swept into the pool, mostly held their positions and kept chanting.

Shaking her head to free herself from Mestizer's hypnotic gaze, Emily thought for a brief instant that they'd won. But Mestizer simply stretched her back and smiled.

'Try to stop me? Yes, my dear, I realised that, I realised that all along.' Mestizer rolled out her arm toward the remaining water-soaked pile of kindling, as if unfurling a scroll. At once, despite the water, the pile burst into furious flames of gold, silver and bronze.

Cionadh started to scream, but by the time the sound made its way to his mouth, most of his flesh had been consumed by the unnatural fire.

'But *you* have to realise,' said Mestizer, still smiling, 'that you're entirely too late.'

CHAPTER 13

Emily could scarcely take in what happened next. The ebon statue suddenly began to glow with light, brighter and brighter, until it hurt her eyes to keep looking at it. But still she could not tear her gaze away. And as she watched, the figure also started to grow bigger – much bigger – until it almost filled the entire chamber.

Eventually the dazzling radiance faded, and the demon stood crouched before them, no longer fixed in the form of a statue, but very much alive. What had once been a group Mind, a complex mass of thought housed piecemeal across the bodies of an entire species, now had in its own singular, gargantuan body, wedged into a space that seemed tiny by comparison, although it had just recently held over a hundred individuals.

Uncertain of its new, corporeal home, the demon foolishly straightened its curved, hairy, powerful back, sending its head straight up through concrete and steel support girders. Shocked, cut and bruised, it quickly resumed a crouched, almost foetal position, pulling its huge hands in, prodding at its wounds with index fingers several feet long.

'Still! Still!' Mestizer cried, trying desperately to attract the demon's attention. 'You must be careful! You're not used to having a body!'

Lechasseur had by now managed to regain his footing on the ledge by the entrance to the chamber. 'Why'd you conjure that thing into such a small space?' he called down to Mestizer.

Mestizer whirled round. 'Fool! I didn't realise it was going to be this big! The ancient tongues in which these spells are written are difficult to decipher!'

'And you're calling other people fools?' Emily snapped back.

Before Mestizer could respond, the giant shifted, sending huge chunks of stone crashing down to the flooded floor. Mestizer looked at her creation in something akin to horror, clearly not sure what to do next. Then she closed her eyes, took three calming breaths, smiled pleasantly and opened them again.

'Not a problem. We will stay calm. We will succeed.' Edging along the wall like a long black spider, Mestizer pulled herself up next to Emily, then snatched up a chunk of her dark hair in a fist.

Emily cried out in pain and tried to wrench herself free.

'Quiet!' hissed Mestizer. 'This will take only a minute, then my creation and I will be gone.'

The white-skinned woman turned back to the dark, squirming monster and held out her free hand to it, palm up.

'My hand, darling,' Mestizer called to the beast. 'Just touch it. Go ahead. Otherwise, you'll be left behind! This way, we'll leave together and reappear elsewhere in this stupid child's life. I've already picked a spot! A nice green field. A park. Kensington Gardens two weeks ago. A beautiful cloudy night! We'll be outside, you and I. Then we can plan!'

'You can pick where to go?' Lechasseur asked, voicing the same question that had popped into Emily's head.

Mestizer turned to him briefly, shook her head and said only: 'Tch.'

Then her focus was back on the giant. 'Do you understand? Just touch my hand! We'll leave your subjects to feast on these two!'

The giant, if anything less human in appearance than the Subterraneans, nevertheless watched Mestizer as she spoke. Now, perhaps unwilling to ram its head upward again, and sensing little other alternative, it seemed to want to obey. It looked at her tiny fingers, then at its own huge hand, then back at her again.

Mestizer nodded, frantically, excitedly. 'Yes! Yes! Your hand!' She held her own hand out, rubbed it, fanned the fingers, then pointed toward its colossal appendages. 'You're not unintelligent! I know! Just a little disorientated! I can help that! I can make you understand faster! Just give me your hand!'

A spark lit in twin brown corneas the size of manhole covers. The demon King shifted its shoulder, loosening the ceiling still further. A chunk of reinforced concrete the size of a motor car hit the wall barely two feet away from Lechasseur, then smashed into the pool below, its surface forming a small island in the swirling muck.

Then the King slowly stretched its arm out towards Mestizer.

The woman was beside herself. 'Yes!' she cried. 'Yes!'

As if sensing something was about to happen, but not realising it would mean the disappearance of their King, the Subterraneans began to hoot, growl and jump up and down excitedly, apparently returning to their more bestial state.

The huge neo-simian hand moved steadily closer to that of the eager, black-clad woman. Mestizer stretched forward, pulling Emily's hair tightly, making her scream again, as she tried to reduce the distance between her and her goal.

Lechasseur knew that he and Emily wouldn't survive ten minutes with the Subterraneans if Mestizer and the giant vanished, to say nothing of what would happen in Kensington Park when they arrived. As his leather coat flopped wetly against him, he again worried that it would never be the same. But an open fold at the pocket gave him a glimpse of the extra electric torch, and, more importantly, the spare chocolate bar.

He slid out the bar. Soggy from the sewer water, it half-clung to the pocket's lining. Using his fingernails, which he was grateful he hadn't clipped in a while, he scraped the paper off, then held it aloft and began calling: 'Here! Here!'

If he could get the Subterraneans to see it, or smell it, the ensuing rush might give him and Emily a chance to escape.

At first, everyone ignored him, even Emily. The collected eyes were all trained on the vanishing distance between the King's and Mestizer's hands. Lechasseur yelled louder and longer, finally pricking the ears, not of the Subterraneans, Mestizer or Emily, but of the unholy King.

Freezing its hand a few feet from Mestizer's, it sniffed the air, then rolled its eyes toward Lechasseur. It knew what it was smelling. It knew that it was good. It knew that it should have it.

Lechasseur's own eyes went wide with terror as the huge thing began to try to force its way bodily toward him, crushing stone and luckless Subterraneans as it went. Without thinking, just as Mestizer and Emily were turning to see what the giant was reaching for, Lechasseur hurled the chocolate bar at the King.

It raised both its hands to try to catch it, sending stone and iron support beams raining down. But, of course, its over-sized fingers were hopelessly ill-equipped for the job of snatching a tiny rectangle from mid-air, and it failed.

The bar bounced off its chest, then tumbled down along its oily skin. It fell through the air into the whirlpool of muck on the floor, where it was quickly sucked below the surface.

Not understanding why it had been denied what it wanted, the King flew into a rage. It raised its hands through stone and masonry, kicked its feet down through the solid floor.

As the walls and floor swayed and began to shatter utterly, the Subterraneans skittered away, and Emily used the opportunity to knee Mestizer hard in the side. Caught off guard, the stronger, more powerful woman released her grip and found herself slipping down to the small concrete island in the centre of the pool.

'YOU!' Mestizer bellowed, grabbing her hurt side with one hand, pointing the white-skinned index finger of the other at Emily.

But Emily could barely hear her above the chaos. The floor cracked beneath her as the mad King continued trying pull itself up into freedom. More debris tumbled into a widening pit. One minute Mestizer had the block of dislodged stone beneath her feet, the next it had shifted and there was nothing holding her up but her anger and will. The last thing Mestizer shrieked before disappearing into the whirlpool of cracked stone, concrete and sewage was: 'If only I'd met you sooner! This is all *your* fault!'

Then she, along with most of the room, was gone.

Delighted, the Subterraneans hooted and howled, gracefully leaping from one part of the falling walls to another. Some were crushed in mid-celebratory grunt. Others dared actually climb atop their mighty King – who seemed to have as little regard for them as it did for Mestizer, and shook them away as it might uncomfortable drops of sweat.

Finding a series of foot- and handholds, Emily managed to climb to Lechasseur's side. As the Subterraneans dived, chattered, screamed and died in a frenzy before their King, Emily and Lechasseur reached what was left of the entrance tunnel, then clawed, stumbled and half-ran out as quickly as they could.

A roar of shattering sewer, coupled with intermittent sub-human howls, followed them as they lurched through the hellish darkness, each praying that the other remembered the way out.

'I think it's here!'

'Are you sure?'

'I feel the rungs!'

Minutes later, they threw open a manhole cover and emerged into a more familiar, more human night. But it was not to remain familiar. As Emily and Lechasseur stumbled along the deserted street, the King's arms breached the buckled tarmac. Then its full mass clambered up into the cool night air, the bodies of several of its subjects crushed flat against its torso. Howling, it swung its arms left and right, fingers scraping the sides of buildings on either side of the street.

'So what happened to your Carl Jung theory?' Lechasseur asked Emily. 'I thought the hive Mind was supposed to be brilliant! This 'thing is acting like a refugee from a horror film!'

Emily shrugged. 'It's used to seeing the world in four dimensions, through hundreds of eyes! I guess it's maddening to be stuck in one body with three dimensions.'

As the creature stretched, the top of its head rose up above the roofs of some nearby four-storey buildings. Emily and Lechasseur realised for the first time that it must be over a hundred feet tall.

Perhaps simply because it had been stuck in any body at all, the King was still very, very angry. With a howl that shook the windows in the surrounding buildings, the King started smashing at the walls with his fists. A few more blows and it looked as if a whole building might come down straight on top of Emily and Lechasseur.

'We've got to get to Crest!' Emily shouted.

CHAPTER 14

Hurtling bits of grey and black concrete mingled with giant swathes of hairy ape flesh as Emily and Lechasseur tumbled and ran in search of cover.

'Crest?' Lechasseur called, his damp leather coat flapping against him in a series of small thwacks as he raced along. He sounded vaguely disappointed to hear the name again.

'Of course,' Emily answered, only a few steps ahead. 'Don't tell me you haven't guessed yet? It's why we were drawn to him from the start. He's the centre of all this.'

'Actually, I haven't guessed anything of the sort,' Lechasseur growled.

An animal yowl made him look back over his shoulder. The King was beating his head with his fisted hands, as if trying to crack open his huge skull and free his mind from its new bondage. The hands tore hair, raked leathery skin, but still the King didn't seem to understand why it hurt so much.

Lechasseur found himself slowing as he stared, then coming to a full halt. Emily was ten yards ahead before she noticed he wasn't beside her.

'What is it?' she called back. She took a few more steps from momentum, then stopped herself. 'This really isn't the time to take in the sights.'

'It's . . . strange,' Lechasseur said, realising how silly he sounded as he spoke.

'Yes, a giant ape is trashing the buildings! Now, come on!' she shouted, waving him frantically forward. She was about to run towards him, with the thought of pulling him along with her forcibly, when a piece of building, half the size of a car, crashed onto the road between them.

The King, head bloody from the pounding he'd given himself, had turned to taking out his frustration on the buildings.

'Honoré?' she cried. 'Now would be good!'

But the tall black man could not comply. Something in his mind, in the darker reaches of his psyche that he dreaded, was forcing him to stare at the nightmarish behemoth. For a moment it seemed to Lechasseur that there was not one, but two Kings, then three, then four, then a whole blur of them, mixing into a rolling, hairy brown tentacle.

Worms. He was seeing those damn worms that crawled into and out of the ether, careening, spilling into past and future, heedless of the nice, clean boundaries that normally stood between the two. In one direction, the past, the King worm rippled back down into the street, below, into the sewers where it had been born. But in the other direction, the future, it wrapped its way through London, leaving wreckage and corpses in its wake.

Overcoming her fright, Emily scrambled around the debris and came up to Honoré, her eyes narrowing as she saw the open, blank expression on his face.

'You're seeing things, aren't you?' she asked. 'Things about the King?'

Lechasseur nodded once.

Nearby, the front of a four-story building rattled as the King placed his hands on the roof, braced his considerable feet against the first floor, and pulled. The building came down, a raging torrent of bricks, rock and plaster that slammed into and rolled along the street. If anyone had been inside, they'd smartly fled at the first pounding.

Rather than tear at the rest of the building, the King walked forward, into it, as if it shouldn't be there and he could simply slip through it. When its undeniable physicality rebuffed him, he howled, then stepped automatically back into it, like a hundred foot tall wind-up toy whose spring driven motor kept dumbly slamming it into the same wall over and over again.

It was an odd dance – funny, really, if not for the rubble that continued to fall.

'He's trying to get to something in that direction,' Lechasseur said numbly. 'He hasn't figured out he can walk around it yet. He will in a minute, then he'll take off down the street.'

True to Lechasseur's prediction, after the fourth or fifth attempt to walk through the building, the King stepped back. He raised his moon-sized eyes over the rooftops, flared his nostrils, then turned and started awkwardly moving his Brobdingnagian legs along the easier, trench-like spaces.

His massive back was to Emily and Lechasseur. They, at least, were safe for the moment. Then Emily grabbed Lechasseur's arm and pulled, not away, but toward the creature.

Lechasseur yanked his hand back as if she were on fire. 'Are you mad?' he asked.

'He's looking for Crest, isn't he? We'll jump to Crest,' she said, grabbing at his hand again. 'Mestizer can do it, so can we!'

'She's had more practice,' Lechasseur said, snapping his hand this way and that to avoid her touch.

'Concentrate on what you're seeing, we'll both think of Crest! I'm sure it'll work!' Emily said.

'Are you? Are you sure?' Lechasseur objected.

'Well, no, but it's worth a try,' she said. 'It seemed to work before . . .' She feinted left with her shoulder, then jutted to the right at a bare patch of air just as Lechasseur moved his hand there. She couldn't tell whether he'd agreed, or she'd just managed to move a little faster than he, but in any event, their hands met, and neither let go as the veil of perception most people confused for the greater world, quickly twisted, shimmered and burst in a kaleidoscope of blue lightning.

Then, almost as quickly as it happened, the chaos of overwhelming sensations sorted itself back into order. The hospital came into view. They felt their hands still locked tightly to one another.

Orientating herself, Emily quickly realised *where* they were, but *when* was it? An endless crashing, like the rush of war, mixed with screams and a few sirens, turned them both away from the building, toward the street, where the great head of the King poked between the buildings. He was close and coming closer.

'An hour?' Lechasseur muttered. His head was spinning, and the feeling of disorientation he remembered from his last trip through space and time was back with a vengeance. 'We couldn't have jumped more than an hour. It was so fast.'

'It doesn't matter. He'll be here soon. We've got to move.' Emily already had his hand in hers, so she simply tugged him along. He followed, sluggishly at first, but as his mind settled into place, his legs started pumping, and then they ran, together.

'Crest it is,' he said.

They burst through the hospital doors and headed for the central desk. In the lobby, the lights flickered. The King had knocked out the main power lines, leaving the emergency generators to provide what they could. Other than the flashing lights, the interior of the hospital looked like a pocket of order amidst the chaos.

A burly porter, temples greying, stepped into Lechasseur's path, his hand held up.

'We need to see Randolph Crest, immediately!' Lechasseur commanded. His arrogant tone reminded Emily of something she'd nearly forgotten. Lechasseur was, despite his attempts at cultivating an English accent and an English air, an American from New Orleans. Unfortunately, the porter noted the fact as well.

'Are you an immediate family member, sir?' the porter asked.

'No, but . . .'

'Can I assume you are not a doctor?'

'Yes, but it's crucial . . .' Lechasseur began.

The porter nodded over his shoulder at a throng of doctors and nurses engaged in desperate life-saving efforts around a group of stretcher-borne patients. 'As you can see, sir, there are many vital activities taking place at the moment. Immediate family and hospital staff only.'

Lechasseur began to pace in frustration. Emily rolled her eyes.

'I need to see him immediately!'

'Might I suggest, sir, that you return home, shower and acquire some proper clothing. By the time you return, the situation may well be under control.'

Unable to contain his frustration any longer, Lechasseur brought the conversation to an abrupt end by punching the porter in the mouth and sending him sprawling to the floor.

A woman at the reception desk blanched as the tall, imposing Negro loomed over her. 'Randolph Crest,' said Lechasseur levelly. 'Which room?'

The receptionist nervously checked her ledger. 'Ward 10, third floor,' she stammered.

Lechasseur tipped his hand at her. 'Thank you.'

The stairwell muffled the approach of the King a little, but as soon as they entered the hallway of the third floor the sounds of smashing masonry and screaming people struck them like a physical force coming through the open windows.

Nurses and doctors hurried about, and Emily smiled and nodded to them as they passed. Lechasseur paid no attention. He rapidly scanned the doors leading off the hallway until he saw the one leading to Ward 10, then crashed through it into the room beyond.

Crest didn't notice them at first. He was sprawled on his back in the bed nearest the door, his swollen belly forming a large mound under the white sheets, an intravenous line leading from a needle taped to the oily skin of his hand to a glass bottle of some sort of medicine. His head was turned toward the window, giving him a perfect view of the carnage outside.

Lechasseur and Emily took a second to look outside as well. The King was approaching fast.

'End of the light! End of the light!' Crest cried in his high-pitched voice, now more frantic than it had ever been.

Instantly, Lechasseur's thoughts were tugged by the same strong longing that had struck the first time he'd seen Crest. Much as he hated time travel, there was something in this man's, this creature's, life that his instincts were begging to see.

'Let's get this over with,' Lechasseur said. He grabbed Emily's hand and they stepped forward together.

A combined shriek from Crest and the creature outside made them pause. With a surprising burst of energy, Crest rolled out of the bed away from them, briefly revealing a dark, hairy back, the same colour as those of the Subterraneans. The drip pulled from his hand and he scooted away. Cornered between the window and the bed, he faced the two friends, his eyes rolling wildly. His body no longer fully his own, he was fighting to stay in control of himself.

Emily took half a step forward. 'We know you're one of them,' she said. 'That's why you're connected to the hive Mind. That's what made you think they were after you!'

'It's more than that! They *were* after me! And now *it* is!!' Crest yelled.

Seeing no exit, he began to panic. His hands shook, his legs wobbled and ripples ran through his loose flesh. 'The light is ending!' he said again. 'I should have guessed you would be the ones to bring it to me!'

Lechasseur and Emily both took a step towards him. He cowered and covered his face. Outside, the King did the same.

'You don't understand!' Crest whined, pleading like a lost child. 'I wouldn't stay with them anymore! I couldn't stay with them anymore! They don't speak! They don't think! They don't feel!'

Imagining a space between them that might somehow lead to freedom, he lurched forward, eyes wild and reeling, pain mutating into anger, adrenaline pumping through his veins. Through the window behind him, they could see the King repeat the action, careening into the side of a building, sending a torrent of rubble down to the street below.

'Who controls whom?' Emily said.

'Does it matter?' Lechasseur answered, pulling her forward another step.

'I won't!' Crest howled. 'And I don't care if London and all the rest of your damned human cities *are* destroyed!'

Lechasseur shrugged. 'But we do,' he said.

With that, he closed the distance and grabbed Crest's right arm.

Lechasseur realised in a flash how right his instincts had been. Crest's entire being was now rolling out before him. The spot on his hand that touched Emily's was crackling with the vibrant feeling of electricity. Blue lightning flickered around them as the power grew.

The world of things in which there could be objects that sat next to one another, collided into meaninglessness. The whirl that Lechasseur saw as he breached the known rules of existence, briefly revealed to him the smallest edges of the great single Event that truly comprised the totality of being. Then it all rushed backwards in a dreadful flood.

Lechasseur already hated this part.

CHAPTER 15

Rush of white light, rush of colour, then a tumble into shades of black. Lechasseur felt heat all around him, close – if possible, solid – air. He was dizzy, just like the first time he'd leapt through time and space, and he'd wound up somewhere in a field. This time, he knew what had happened, he'd been ready for it, he'd wanted it to happen. But as much as he told himself this, his senses remained doggedly confused. The image of the hospital room and the surreal destruction visible outside its window were still too fresh to relinquish for the sake of the muddy blackness that now greeted his eyes. It was as though he'd been caught half-awake and was now unable to decide which was real and which was dream.

Emily's harsh, insistent whisper helped.

'Honoré? Honoré? Are you there?'

Emily was apparently used to this sort of travel. How this could be, Lechasseur had no idea; the secrets were locked in her amnesia. But he could hear in her tone that she was worried, nevertheless. From the sound of her voice, she couldn't be more than a few yards away, but he could see nothing in the darkness. Unless he really was dreaming. Then she might as well be on another planet.

'Honoré?' Her voice was louder, more concerned.

'Here,' he finally said, deciding she was real, or the next best thing.

He heard her feet move along a hard, uneven surface. Then he felt her hand brush his chest and come to rest firmly on his shoulder.

'Where are we?' Lechasseur asked, lowering his voice to a whisper, lest something in the dark might hear.

'Somewhere in Crest's past,' she answered, equally hushed. 'Underground, I think.'

'Crest is one of those things,' Lechasseur said. 'Should have guessed from the start. But he did look different. More . . . human, I guess.'

'That's because he's spent a lifetime trying to fit in with us,' Emily said, 'and because he was never *just* one of them. Remember what Mestizer said about their King? What Crest himself said he was? A rare born, smarter than the others, born to lead, or at least to focus the hive Mind.'

Lechasseur immediately understood. 'He left them because he couldn't stand it.'

Emily said nothing, but Lechasseur somehow sensed her nodding in agreement.

'So where is he?' Lechasseur asked. He turned about, trying in vain to make out their surroundings. 'Can't imagine why someone would want to leave all this.'

Sweat had accumulated on his upper lip and was running down towards his mouth. He spat it away by pressing some air between his pursed lips. At the end of his breath, a touch of coolness graced his mouth.

'Feel that?' he whispered, stepping toward the coolness. 'A breeze.'

He felt her press her face forward, although she kept her hand firmly on his shoulder.

'It's coming from here,' she said.

He groped forward, she beside him, still touching, as his fingers probed stone and dirt walls. His hand soon found the source of the breeze, hidden behind a large boulder wedged near the top of the space they were in. It was a narrow crevice, a space heading upwards. The rocks of which it was composed were anything but steady. Even the slight pressure from his hand sent pebbles and earth clattering down.

'Move carefully,' Lechasseur cautioned. 'We don't want to start a cave-in.'

'Do you still have your torch?' she asked, recalling the second one in his pocket.

'Yes, of course,' Lechasseur said, mentally kicking himself that he hadn't thought of this himself. He withdrew it and flipped the switch, starkly revealing the natural browns and greys of the space they were in.

'Point it up there, please,' Emily said.

Lechasseur hesitated, then obeyed, angling the light toward the crevice, and beyond. For a second, despite the power from the new batteries, the light found nothing. Then, it fell on a patch of lighter rock, almost white and squared at the edges.

'Concrete,' Lechasseur said. 'The bottom of a building foundation. Or a sewer, or the tube. The Subterraneans were trapped down here until that bomb blast last week, but Crest found a way out decades ago. This is what started it all. Maybe we do . . .'

Before he could finish the sentence, Lechasseur felt his still-sore jaw snap sideways under terrific pressure from something fast, oily and hairy. The torch fell from his hand as his head slammed sideways into the wall, dislodging a few more stones.

As Lechasseur tumbled, the Subterranean leapt atop him, snapping vile teeth toward his face. Lechasseur rolled sideways just in time to avoid losing his chin, his greater weight throwing the thing off balance. It toppled, righted itself, then bounced off a far wall and braced itself for a leap. With a dread chattering, the thing was on him again, tearing fingernails into his face, digging into his coat near his abdomen with prehensile feet.

Lechasseur raised his hands and his legs, trying to fend off the brutal attack. Thinking his back a less vulnerable target, his panicked mind was trying to figure out how best to roll over when a dull THUD filled the air. No longer attacking, the creature slumped off him into the dark.

'Honoré! Honoré! Say something!' he heard Emily cry. 'I just hit one of you on the head with a rock, and I'm not sure which! Honoré?'

'Here,' he moaned, then slowly started getting back to his feet. She helped him up as best she could on the jagged terrain. He could feel with his hands that there was some blood on his face, but none seemed to be flowing. Perhaps he'd got away with just scratches and bruises.

'Just like Cionadh,' he mused. 'Do some things in time always repeat?'

'I suppose,' Emily said. 'Like ritual.'

The glowing torch had rolled downhill a bit, so he scrambled after it, then shone the light on his wounded attacker. The dark, hairy chest moved steadily up and down, indicating it was still alive. A large bump rose on the left side of its skull where Emily had struck with the stone. As if it sensed the light, the creature tried to rise briefly. Lechasseur tensed. But then it lapsed into complete unconsciousness.

'That's a particularly ugly specimen,' Lechasseur said, noting the oily flesh that hung so loosely on its frame. All at once, something in the creature's face struck him as familiar. 'Sweet heaven,' he exclaimed. 'This is Crest!'

'This must be the moment in his life when he found the passage,' Emily said. 'This is the moment we were both being drawn to all along.'

Lechasseur was about to agree, when a new sound made him whirl. A low, familiar scraping and shuffling made its way up from a lower darkness. Even in the few seconds that he stood listening, it grew slowly but unmistakably louder.

'It's the others!' Emily said, whispering again. 'They're probably looking for him!'

'I know how to fix this,' Lechasseur said. He suspected Emily had guessed as well, but voiced it anyway. 'If this passage weren't here, Crest never would have left the underworld. All we have to do is seal it off.'

He let the torch light glance once more on the creature's unconscious form. Emily looked as well. Without the wrinkles and ripples that reflected the anxiety of conscious thought, for the first time the face seemed quite peaceful.

'Seems a bit cruel to trap him here forever with those things,' Emily said. 'He is a poet.'

Lechasseur turned back to the upward passage. 'As cruel as letting him be killed by a so-called King in his hospital bed? To mention nothing of the tally of four sacrificial victims, and who knows how many others at the hands of the King?'

Still, an undeniable twinge of regret accompanied his decision. Though he could think of no other parallels between them, Lechasseur knew that Crest was an outsider like himself. That alone made him feel for the creature's plight. But what else could he do? Feel angry and guilty the way Emily did?

A sudden memory caught him off guard. He was in Dorset, 1943, on leave, sitting in a café with some of the soldiers from his company. They were talking about all the changes wrought to the world by one man: Adolph Hitler.

As he recalled, Lechasseur had, without really intending to, turned the conversation by asking, out of nowhere: 'What if they'd known what Hitler would do before he came to power, and they could have stopped it all with a single bullet to his head?'

At the time, it was for Lechasseur a stray, aberrant notion. Only now did he realise that it may have been an early twinge of what he was eventually to become.

Most of his friends were delighted at the wish-fulfilment fantasy, and went on to describe in some gruesome detail what exactly they would do to the proto-Fuhrer. Then their officer, Lt Jerome Friedman, an educated man, simply shrugged and said: 'Would you really condone killing Hitler when he was a child? Would you put your gun to an innocent's head?'

The memory ended, but its taste lingered in Lechasseur's mind. He looked back down at Crest, realising that he was about to condemn him to the darkness. But this was no thought experiment. The Subterraneans were approaching, and Lechasseur wasn't killing anyone. In fact, he'd be saving quite a few people. And who knew how long a life, or of exactly what kind, Crest would have down here?

A nagging feeling in Lechasseur's belly suggested that, in spite of his inner denials, he knew the answer to that last question, but he forced it away.

There was no real choice.. If Emily, always the more humanist of the two, had any objections, she wasn't voicing them.

Lechasseur felt along the heavier rocks that made up the entrance to the passage. A good shove would send them, and probably a great many more, down to seal the gap. He braced himself and grunted as he pushed, hoping to beat the arrival of the others.

'Wait!' Emily shouted, grabbing his shoulder again.

'What?' Lechasseur spat back, annoyed. 'Forget about Crest! We don't have a choice!'

'No. I know we have to do it. But don't you think we'd be better off on the *other* side of the tunnel? If this works, Crest will never reach the surface, and we'll still be surrounded by Subterraneans. I suppose we might be able to use one to jump back to our own time, but that's assuming they don't catch us and use us to help with their protein deficiency.'

'Right,' Lechasseur answered.

Together, they scrambled through the small opening, where the air was even cooler. Beyond the section of visible concrete, they could even see a far-off light.

Again, Lechasseur braced himself, and this time, invigorated slightly by the fresher air, pushed for all he was worth. With a rumble, a large rock, and several of the smaller ones on which he and Emily were standing, slid free of whatever had been holding them back and tumbled forward. Lechasseur fell, dropping the torch. It clattered down into the lower tunnel, then vanished in a landslide of rock and dust. As Lechasseur rolled about, he had no idea what was happening to Emily, but hoped she'd found a better hand-hold than he.

When the rumbling finally died away, and the dust settled, she appeared at once by his side, her breathing only slightly heavier than it had been. They felt about with their hands. The pile of rock now in front of them was really quite impressive.

No-one's digging through that with their bare hands, Lechasseur thought. *No matter how much their heart desires.*

CHAPTER 16

The flat was strewn with the newspapers they'd collected from the last several weeks. Emily and Lechasseur, enjoying some hot tea, diligently scanned one after the other, trying to piece together the changes they'd wrought.

It'd been easy enough to determine that although the bomb blast had occurred, and the life of Lt Clive Gidley had still been lost, there'd been no subsequent raids on the streets of London by creatures sub-human or otherwise. All the damage they'd witnessed in the streets was likewise gone, or rather, had never taken place. The major issues out of the way, they concentrated on the subtleties.

Upon climbing up through the tunnel, they had reached the lively Constitution Hill tube station, and then the pre-war streets of London. From there, it had been a simple matter to find a young woman whose life extended to early 1950, and whom they could use to make the jump home. Lechasseur had picked her out fairly quickly from a crowd, and intuited the right time to jump to almost at once. He was pleased that his control over his abilities seemed to be growing. Even the subsequent dizziness had been less this time.

'Here's an advert for Bungard's poetry readings,' Emily said. 'No mention of Randolph Crest attending.' She had to squint to read the advert in the dim light of the flat. Though it was mid-morning, the curtains remained drawn. She was too exhausted to challenge Honoré today.

Noticing, and feeling in an atypically gregarious mood, he rose and opened the curtains himself. The morning fog had yet to lift completely, but even the overcast sky alleviated the darkness in the room.

'Sick of the dark?' Emily asked.

Lechasseur shook his head as he lifted his cup from the end table. 'Not really.' But then he added, looking outside: 'Maybe just for today.'

'Of course, you realise, Mestizer is still alive,' Emily added. She briefly thought of sweetening her own tea, then decided to use lemon instead. Knowing Honoré had some perks.

'At least she won't remember you,' Lechasseur offered.

Emily turned to him. 'Don't be so certain. You and I have so far remembered the alternate time lines we've visited, haven't we?'

Lechasseur furrowed his brow. He made his hands flat, like a pair of scales, then moved them up and down as he spoke, weighing the choices. 'Still . . . Mestizer. London. London. Mestizer.'

It wasn't the greatest joke in the world, but Emily didn't even seem to be listening.

'Something else on your mind?' he asked.

'Yes. It's just that the V1 still exploded,' she said. 'So the path to their underworld, or whatever you want to call it, must still have opened. Why wouldn't they want to come up from that dreadful place even *with* their rare-born king?'

'Habit,' Lechasseur theorised. 'Or, stopping Crest somehow stopped them as well.'

Thinking of Crest brought a twinge of remorse to Lechasseur. Now, in the fullness of time, just as Emily had second-guessed their ability to save Windleby, ways of saving the poet, ways of saving them all, had occurred to him. Maybe they could have brought Crest up with them, moved him to another continent? Or perhaps they could have somehow helped Gidley, stopped the bomb from exploding? There must be something they could go back and do or undo that might make things better. Maybe next time he would be better able to finesse things.

He furrowed his brow, somewhat disturbed that he'd even acknowledged there would be a next time. But Emily was right. Remorse was a different creature when you could hop through time.

Out of nowhere, Emily started humming the same catchy tune she'd hummed about a week ago, its source, like the lines of time they travelled, still utterly unknown. It lightened his heart a bit. He found himself wondering where she'd learned it, and if he might someday see Emily's home for himself.

Outside the window, Lechasseur saw a tall man being dragged along the streets by a small white poodle. A glimpse of the man's future showed that the dog would soon be peeing on his new shoes. For some reason, this struck Lechasseur as funny, and he smiled for the first time in days.

Even with the fog, or perhaps because of it, it looked like it was going to be a beautiful day.

EPILOGUE

I had light once, for a time.

Upon waking from a dream, I found it, rushing out from the end of a stick. I grabbed the stick and I held it tightly, the way I once tried to hold my secret thoughts.

The others were coming, fearing I had fled; worse, fearing that I had found some sweetness that they would be unable to share. I had found sweetness, but not the kind they lusted for. As they came, I showed it to them, shone it on them, and saw all their huddled faces for the first and last time. And I realised how much they looked like me.

Exposed, stabbed by the light, they howled and screamed, louder even than the shouts they gave whenever the sweetness was passed around. Then they fled, the way the dark itself fled from my light.

Then I was alone, as I had wanted, with the light I had dreamed of. I leapt with it, I howled with it. I shone it against the walls of the world. I chased the others with it, showing them power they never expected, even from their king.

But when I tired, and curled up on the rough ground, clinging to the stick, they would no longer sleep with me. I missed the feel of their breath, the sound of hearts beating other than my own. I dreamt of their faces, all the same as each other, all the same as mine.

When I woke, the stick was still in my hands, but the light had emptied from it.

Still, in my mind, I could see the faces of the others. It was then I realised that I'd been wrong. The darkness comforts. The darkness suffices.

Light may be only a relic from a time when there were things worth seeing.

Words may be from a time when there were things worth saying.

And my longing may have been from a time when there were things to want.

By leaving, the light gave me something else. It gave me memory.

And memory gave a new thing as well: a tasteless, textureless, odourless thing that passes constantly through us all, a thing that ages, decays and withers even the rocks that form the walls of the world. It is this thing, that by and by took the fires of my early days and brought all my yearnings to a comfortable sameness.

There is food here. There is warmth. There has been much mating and I have sired many children, only some of which we have been forced to eat. Here all things are, and here all must remain.

And until I fade into this thing that passes through all of us, until I can rise from my nest no more, and the others will perhaps take me into their bellies, I will want no other world.

What for?

I have no need of words.

Once, for a time, I had light.

And now I know I will always have time.

ABOUT THE AUTHOR

A professional writer of comics, novels and scripts for well over a decade, Stefan Petrucha most recently sold his first feature script, *Grace of God*, commissioned by director Allen Rubin. His spec screenplay *Lance Barnes: Post Nuke Dick*, based on his original comic property, currently has Matt Frewer (Max Headroom) attached to star. Petrucha also currently writes dark fantasy novels for White Wolf Publishing and comic books for Moonstone Books. His first vampire novel, *Dark Ages: Assamite* received many rave reviews and has gone into a second printing.

His latest comic, *Kolchak: Devil in the Details* is already being hailed as a classic in the series. In fact, Jeff Rice, creator of the cult TV hit *Kolchak: The Night Stalker*, was so pleased with Petrucha's script, he felt it should be used as the template for all future *Kolchak* scripts, and at one point enthused in his notes, 'This scene is . . . well . . . literature. It has genuine substance very neatly handled. Take care. This kind of thing could spread and, ohmigawd, "elevate" the comic novel a rung or two.'

Internationally acclaimed as the scribe of Topp's *X-Files* comic book, Petrucha's work on that series has been republished in six trade paperbacks in the US and abroad. He's also scripted over 100 comic book adventures for Mickey Mouse & Donald Duck for Egmont Publishing in Denmark, which have been published in over 35 languages.

He is also the writer/creator of such comic book characters as *Squalor*, *Meta-4*, *Counterparts* and *The Bandy Man*, and has completed a gaggle of eclectic, top-notch writing assignments. WWW.PETRUCHA.COM

TIME HUNTER

A range of high-quality, original paperback novellas featuring the adventures in time of Honoré Lechasseur. Part mystery, part detective story, part dark fantasy, part science fiction . . . these books are guaranteed to enthral fans of good fiction everywhere, and are in the spirit of our acclaimed range of *Doctor Who* Novellas.

ALREADY AVAILABLE:

THE WINNING SIDE by LANCE PARKIN
Emily is dead! Killed by an unknown assailant. Honoré and Emily find themselves caught up in a plot reaching from the future to their past, and with their very existence, not to mention the future of the entire world, at stake, can they unravel the mystery before it is too late?
An adventure in time and space.
£7.99 (+ £1.50 UK p&p) Standard p/b ISBN 1-903889-35-9 (pb)
£25.00 (+ £1.50 UK p&p) Deluxe h/b ISBN 1-903889-36-7 (hb)

COMING SOON:

THE CLOCKWORK WOMAN by CLAIRE BOTT
Honoré and Emily find themselves imprisoned in the 19th Century by a celebrated inventor . . . but help comes from an unexpected source – a humanoid automaton created by and to give pleasure to its owner. As the trio escape to London, they are unprepared for what awaits them, and at every turn it seems impossible to avert what fate may have in store for the Clockwork Woman.
An adventure in time and space.
£7.99 (+ £1.50 UK p&p) Standard p/b ISBN 1-903889-39-1 (pb)
£25.00 (+ £1.50 UK p&p) Deluxe h/b ISBN 1-903889-40-5 (hb)
PUB: JUNE 2004 (UK)

TIME HUNTER FILM:

DAEMOS RISING by DAVID J HOWE, directed by KEITH BARNFATHER
Daemos Rising is a sequel to both the *Doctor Who* adventure *The Daemons*

and to *Downtime*, an earlier drama featuring the Yeti. It is also a prequel of sorts to Telos Publishing's *Time Hunter* series. It stars Miles Richardson as ex-UNIT operative Douglas Cavendish, and Beverley Cressman as Brigadier Lethbridge-Stewart's daughter Kate. Trapped in an isolated cottage, Cavendish thinks he is seeing ghosts. The only person who might understand and help is Kate Lethbridge-Stewart . . . but when she arrives, she realises that Cavendish is key in a plot to summon the Daemons back to the Earth. With time running out, Kate discovers that sometimes even the familiar can turn out to be your worst nightmare. Also starring Andrew Wisher, and featuring Ian Richardson as the Narrator.

An adventure in time and space.

£12.00 (+ £2.50 UK p&p) VHS; £14.00 (+ £2.50 UK p&p) DVD
Order direct from Reeltime Pictures, PO Box 23435, London SE26 5WU

HORROR/FANTASY

URBAN GOTHIC: LACUNA & OTHER TRIPS ed. DAVID J. HOWE
Stories by Graham Masterton, Christopher Fowler, Simon Clark, Debbie Bennett, Paul Finch, Steve Lockley & Paul Lewis.
Based on the Channel 5 horror series.
SOLD OUT

THE MANITOU by GRAHAM MASTERTON
A 25th Anniversary author's preferred edition of this classic horror novel. An ancient Red Indian medicine man is reincarnated in modern day New York intent on reclaiming his land from the white men.
£9.99 (+ £2.50 UK p&p) Standard p/b ISBN: 1-903889-70-7
£30.00 (+ £2.50 UK p&p) Deluxe h/b ISBN: 1-903889-71-5

CAPE WRATH by PAUL FINCH
Death and horror on a deserted Scottish island as an ancient Viking warrior chief returns to life.
£8.00 (+ £1.50 UK p&p) Standard p/b ISBN: 1-903889-60-X

KING OF ALL THE DEAD by STEVE LOCKLEY & PAUL LEWIS
The king of all the dead will have what is his.
£8.00 (+ £1.50 UK p&p) Standard p/b ISBN: 1-903889-61-8

GUARDIAN ANGEL by STEPHANIE BEDWELL-GRIME

Devilish fun as Guardian Angel Porsche Winter loses a soul to the devil . . .
£9.99 (+ £2.50 UK p&p) Standard p/b ISBN: 1-903889-62-6

ASPECTS OF A PSYCHOPATH by ALISTAIR LANGSTON

Goes deeper than ever before into the twisted psyche of a serial killer.
Horrific, graphic and gripping, this book is not for the squeamish.
£8.00 (+ £1.50 UK p&p) Standard p/b ISBN: 1-903889-63-4

SPECTRE by STEPHEN LAWS

The inseparable Byker Chapter: six boys, one girl, growing up together
in the back streets of Newcastle. Now memories are all that Richard Eden
has left, and one treasured photograph. But suddenly, inexplicably, the
images of his companions start to fade, and as they vanish, so his friends
are found dead and mutilated. Something is stalking the Chapter, picking
them off one by one, something connected with their past, and with
the girl they used to know.
£9.99 (+ £2.50 UK p&p) Standard p/b ISBN: 1-903889-72-3
£30.00 (+ £2.50 UK p&p) Deluxe h/b ISBN: 1-903889-73-1

TV/FILM GUIDES

BEYOND THE GATE: THE UNOFFICIAL AND UNAUTHORISED GUIDE TO STARGATE SG-1 by KEITH TOPPING

Complete episode guide to the middle of Season 6 (episode 121) of the
popular TV show.
£9.99 (+ £2.50 UK p&p) Standard p/b ISBN: 1-903889-50-2

A DAY IN THE LIFE: THE UNOFFICIAL AND UNAUTHORISED GUIDE TO 24 by KEITH TOPPING

Complete episode guide to the first season of the popular TV show.
£9.99 (+ £2.50 p&p) Standard p/b ISBN: 1-903889-53-7

THE TELEVISION COMPANION: THE UNOFFICIAL AND UNAUTHORISED GUIDE TO DOCTOR WHO by DAVID J HOWE & STEPHEN JAMES WALKER

Complete episode guide to the popular TV show.
£14.99 (+ £4.75 UK p&p) Standard p/b ISBN: 1-903889-51-0

LIBERATION: THE UNOFFICIAL AND UNAUTHORISED GUIDE TO BLAKE'S 7 by ALAN STEVENS & FIONA MOORE

Complete episode guide to the popular TV show.
Featuring a foreword by David Maloney
£9.99 (+ £2.50 UK p&p) Standard p/b ISBN: 1-903889-54-5

HOWE'S TRANSCENDENTAL TOYBOX: SECOND EDITION by DAVID J HOWE & ARNOLD T BLUMBERG

Complete guide to *Doctor Who* Merchandise.
£25.00 (+ £4.75 UK p&p) Standard p/b ISBN: 1-903889-56-1

HANK JANSON

Classic pulp crime thrillers from the 1940s and 1950s.

TORMENT by HANK JANSON
£9.99 (+ £1.50 UK p&p) Standard p/b ISBN: 1-903889-80-4
WOMEN HATE TILL DEATH by HANK JANSON
£9.99 (+ £1.50 UK p&p) Standard p/b ISBN: 1-903889-81-2
SOME LOOK BETTER DEAD by HANK JANSON
£9.99 (+ £1.50 UK p&p) Standard p/b ISBN: 1-903889-82-0
SKIRTS BRING ME SORROW by HANK JANSON
£9.99 (+ £1.50 UK p&p) Standard p/b ISBN: 1-903889-83-9

The prices shown are correct at time of going to press. However, the publishers reserve the right to increase prices from those previously advertised without prior notice.

TELOS PUBLISHING

c/o Beech House, Chapel Lane, Moulton, Cheshire, CW9 8PQ, England
Email: orders@telos.co.uk • Web: www.telos.co.uk

To order copies of any Telos books, please visit our website where there are full details of all titles and facilities for worldwide credit card online ordering, or send a cheque or postal order (UK only) for the appropriate amount (including postage and packing), together with details of the book(s) you require, plus your name and address to the above address. Overseas readers please send two international reply coupons for details of prices and postage rates.